Praise for Linwood Barclay

'A devilishly clever, tightly plotted thriller, this grips from the first pages to the superb whip-smart conclusion' *Sunday Mirror*

'This is Barclay firing on all cylinders' *Financial Times*

'This is one of those rare read-at-one-sitting books . . . Barclay is an extremely talented storyteller and a great addition to the crime thriller genre' *Daily Mail*

'A page-turner par excellence' *Sunday Telegraph*

'A fast-moving roller-coaster of a read' *Daily Express*

'Barclay's enjoyably creepy tale . . . certainly keeps one turning the pages' *The Times*

'A gripping web of deception and intrigue'
Woman & Home

'Barclay is the thriller writer everyone's talking about and this book shows why – it's fast and exciting, but with enough substance to the writing to prevent it being slick or shallow' *Morning Star*

'Seamless, breathless and relentlessly pacey, Barclay barely puts a foot wrong' *Daily Mirror*

'A genuinely exciting narrative that will keep readers on tenterhooks . . . once you start, you simply cannot stop reading' *Lady*

'More wriggles and twists than a bag full of snakes . . . mind-blowingly good' *Evening Telegraph*

'A suspense master' Stephen King

Linwood Barclay is married with two children and lives near Toronto. He is a former columnist for the *Toronto Star* and the author of the Richard & Judy 2008 Summer Read winner and number one bestseller *No Time for Goodbye*. To find out more visit www.linwoodbarclay.com

By Linwood Barclay

No Time for Goodbye
Too Close to Home
Fear the Worst
Never Look Away
The Accident
Trust Your Eyes
Never Saw it Coming
A Tap on the Window

Never Saw it Coming

LINWOOD BARCLAY

An Orion paperback

First published in Great Britain in 2013
by Orion
This paperback edition published in 2014
by Orion Books,
an imprint of The Orion Publishing Group Ltd,
Orion House, 5 Upper St Martin's Lane,
London WC2H 9EA

An Hachette UK company

1 3 5 7 9 10 8 6 4 2

A CIP catalogue record for this book
is available from the British Library.

ISBN 978-1-4091-3763-4

Typeset at The Spartan Press Limited,
Lymington, Hants

Printed and bound in Great Britain by
Clays Ltd, St Ives plc

The Orion Publishing Group's policy is to use papers that
are natural, renewable and recyclable products and
made from wood grown in sustainable forests. The logging
and manufacturing processes are expected to conform to
the environmental regulations of the country of origin.

www.orionbooks.co.uk

For Neetha

ONE

"This is ridiculous," Marcia Taggart said. "You're telling me this woman here, just by holding something of Justin's, she's going to be able to figure out where he is? Are you kidding me? She's going to forge some kind of some psychic *link* with him by fondling one of his childhood action figures or wrapping her arms around his pillow? What kind of fool do you take me for?"

"Marcia, for the love of God," said her husband, Dwayne. "If you're not going to call the police, you need to do *something*. For all you know, your boy's in a ditch somewhere. We have to find him."

"You know as well as I do that's probably *exactly* what's happened," Marcia snapped at him. "He's gotten drunk, or high, or he's shacked up with some slut somewhere, or most likely all of the above. If I go running to the police every time he does something like that, we'll need a bigger driveway for all the patrol cars that'll be sitting here all the time."

Keisha Ceylon sat and listened, and watched. Let them have their argument. She could wait.

Dwayne said, "It's been three days. The boy's never been gone this long before."

"That's the problem," Marcia said, pointing an accusing finger at her husband. "You think of him as a boy. He's not a *boy* any more. He's twenty-two and it's time he learned to stand on his own two feet, not waiting around for handouts from his mother. Why do you think I've cut him off? So he'll learn to be responsible, that's why."

Quietly, Dwayne said to her, "I'm not saying you're wrong about any of this. I know what he's put you through. I know it's been hard, raising him on your own after Oscar passed away. I know Justin needs to get his act together. He's a scheming little pain in the ass."

Marcia shot him a look that said, *I can call him that, but you're not his father, so watch it.*

"Sorry," he said, receiving her unspoken message loud and clear. "But I'm not saying anything you haven't said yourself. He can be a handful. But Marcia, just because he's irresponsible doesn't mean he couldn't be in some real trouble." He pointed to the window. A light snow was falling. "It's freezing out there. Suppose you're right. Suppose he did get drunk, or high, and ended up passing out in a snow bank. He could have frozen to death out there. Is that what you want for your own—"

"Of course not!" she shouted. Her lower lip quivered, her eyes glistened.

Here we go, Keisha thought.

"Oh my God," Marcia Taggart said, putting her hands over her face, walking over to the couch and sitting down. She kept her face covered, not wanting her husband, or Keisha, to see her lose control. She plucked a tissue from the box sitting on the coffee table and quickly dabbed her eyes, blew her nose, then sat up very straight. Composed now. Positively regal.

"Well," she said. "So."

Dwayne walked around behind the couch, standing at his wife's back, and rested his hands uneasily on her shoulders. Like he was trying to be comforting, but they were too cold to the touch.

"Even if I accept what you're saying," she said, turning and talking to the hand on her left shoulder to indicate she meant these words for her husband and not their visitor, "why on earth would we turn to this woman for help?"

Still talking like she wasn't there. Keisha knew the type. Before she got into this line of work, when she was cleaning houses for a living—something she still did when money ran short—she'd had clients who treated her like she was a piece of furniture. They'd leave her notes about what they wanted done— "dust TOPS of ceiling fans, wipe stainless-steel sinks dry"—even though she was standing there and they could have told her to her face.

"You won't let me call the police," Dwayne reminded Marcia.

"We've been through this," she snapped. "I just —you know what he's like, what the boy is capable of." She sighed. "Suppose he's fine, but the reason we haven't heard from him is, I don't know, maybe he stole someone's car. Or shoplifted again. Sending the police out to look for him means they'll probably end up charging him with something once they find him. Is that what you want?"

It was Dwayne's turn to sigh. He nodded with false sympathy. "We've called all his friends, we've been to all the places we thought he might be. We're running out of options."

"But *her*?" Marcia tipped her head toward Keisha. "Wouldn't we at least be better off with a private detective?"

Dwayne came around the couch and sat down next to her. "We've been through that, too, Marcia. When I suggested hiring a private eye, you just about bit my head off, because they ask lots of questions like the police would. That's how they work. They have to find the facts, they have to dig them up, they have to talk to lots of people, and that's how everyone gets to know your business, Marcia, and I know how you want to protect Justin, to be discreet about his . . . errors in judgment. But Ms Ceylon here, she doesn't work that way. She *senses* things. She might be able to find out where Justin is without having to stir things up, without having to talk to anyone." He looked at Keisha. "Isn't that right?"

She nodded. "That is the way I work." It was the first time she'd spoken in twenty minutes.

Marcia Taggart shook her head. "But honestly, Dwayne, the woman—really, every New Age psychobabble thing that comes along, you buy into it. This woman—"

"My name," Keisha said, interrupting for the first time, "is Keisha. Keisha Ceylon. I usually answer to

Keisha, but if you'd like to keep referring to me as 'this woman', then I suppose that's your prerogative."

Marcia turned her eyes on her. "I don't believe you can do what you claim to do."

"You would be in the majority," Keisha agreed.

"It's utter nonsense," Marcia said.

"Well, then," Keisha said, standing, "I suppose I should be on my way." She offered up her most sincere smile. "I wish you every success in finding your son."

As she started for the door, Dwayne stood in her path. "Now wait, hang on just a second. Marcia, the woman—Ms Ceylon—went to all the trouble of coming here. I think the least we could do is hear her out."

Marcia snorted. "At what cost?"

Keisha turned to look at the woman, didn't hesitate. "My fee is five thousand dollars." She managed to say it without flinching. It was more than her usual rate, but from what she'd been told, the Taggarts could afford it.

Marcia threw her hands into the air. "Well, there you go, Dwayne. I think we know exactly where this woman's coming from."

"But *only* if I find your son," Keisha added. "If I'm unable to lead you to him, then you pay me absolutely nothing."

That made the room go quiet for several seconds.

"Well, that seems more than fair to me," Dwayne said. "Doesn't that seem fair to you, honey? I mean, come on. Even if you thought this woman was some kind of fraud, how can you lose here?"

Marcia Taggart was thinking and, Keisha guessed, swallowing her pride. Enough to say, "Sit down . . . Ms Ceylon."

Keisha sat back down.

"Just how do you go about this? We turn off the lights, get out a ouija board and start speaking in tongues?"

"No," Keisha said. "Just bring me some of Justin's things. Small, personal items. Things that mattered to him. A sample of his handwriting would be useful, too."

"I can do that," Dwayne said, and left the room hurriedly.

There was an awkward silence between the women. Marcia broke it with, "My husband believes his late mother communicates with him." She accompanied the comment with a roll of the eyes. Telling Keisha she was entertaining this nonsense only to satisfy her husband.

Keisha said nothing.

"He says she gets in touch with him in his dreams, that she calls him from the beyond." The woman made another one of her snorting sounds. "Knowing what a penny-pinching bitch she was, they're probably *collect* calls."

Keisha didn't laugh. She said, "I know you feel a lot of anger toward your son, but I also sense that you love him very much."

"Oh, you sense that, do you?"

6

"Yes, I do. And I know you're actually very worried about him."

"Because of these psychic powers you have?" Marcia asked sarcastically.

"No," Keisha said. "Because I'm a mother. I have a son, too."

Marcia's face softened ever so slightly.

"Matthew. He's ten. And believe me, there are days . . . But no matter what he does, no matter what kind of trouble he gets into at school, I love him. There's nothing he could do that would ever change that. There might be times when I want to wring his neck, but I'd still love him as I was doing it." Keisha smiled. "I'm joking, of course. About wringing his neck."

"No, you don't have to apologize," Marcia said. "Justin, I swear . . . you just want to slap some sense into them."

"I know."

"He's been a handful from the time he could walk, but once he hit his teens, it just got worse. Drinking, drugs, skipping school. I stopped giving him money because I knew he'd just blow it on drugs. But the thing is, this is the part that's so heartbreaking, he's such a *smart* boy."

"I'll bet he is," Keisha said.

"I mean, anything he puts his mind to, he can do it. Computers, he's a whiz with those. He can add up a column of numbers in his head. You say to him, what's four hundred and twenty times six hundred and three, and just like that, he can tell you the answer. He's probably some kind of genius, but instead of using his brain to accomplish something, he's always trying to figure out how to work the system, get some money out of his mother, or"—and she nodded in the direction her husband had gone — "Dwayne. I know he gives Justin money behind my back. He's got a soft spot for him, thinks I'm too tough on him. I think he was so taken with the idea of becoming a father, even a stepfather, that it's blinded him to Justin's faults. The thing is, he's . . . there's something not quite right about Justin. Sometimes he—and this is an awful thing to say, but sometimes he actually kind of scares me. Not physically, but what goes on in that head of his. I just wish . . ."

And then, without warning, tears welled out of her eyes and ran down her cheeks. "Oh, God, I hope nothing's happened to him."

Keisha got out of her chair and sat on the couch next to Marcia Taggart. "It's going to be okay," she said.

"I hope these will do," Dwayne said, coming back into the living room with several items in his hands.

"Put them there," Keisha said, indicating the coffee table, where she had already laid out two of her business cards.

Dwayne set them down gently. An iPod, a paperback copy of the novel *American Psycho*, a cancelled check, a plastic collectible figure of a grotesquely well-endowed woman in superhero garb.

Keisha handled them dubiously. "I'm not sure

8

about—would you have an article of clothing? Something Justin wears regularly? Something that suggests his personality?"

Marcia said, "Get one of his hats." She looked at Keisha. Her eyes were suddenly very weary. "Would a hat work?"

"I think so. In the meantime, let me have a look at these."

Marcia picked up the cancelled check from the things Dwayne had delivered to Keisha and scowled. After a shake of her head, she folded it in half and held it in her fist. With her other hand she picked up the female action figure and studied it as though it were some obscure artifact from an alien civilization.

"Justin collects these things," she said. "I just want to throw them all into the garbage. What's a man in his twenties doing with toys like these? He must have five hundred of them. I don't even know who this is supposed to be. Wonder Woman or—"

"Shh," Keisha said gently, and closed her eyes. She handled the toy, then opened her eyes and picked up the iPod.

"He listens to this a lot," Keisha said.

"He does."

"I can feel . . . when he carries this, it's often in his shirt pocket, right next to his heart," she said.

"Well, I guess that's where lots of people carry them," Marcia said, looking skeptical again. "When you touch his earbuds, are you going to say he wore them right close to his brain?"

Keisha smiled ruefully at the woman. "I thought we were starting to get along."

"All I'm saying is, that was a pretty obvious observation about the iPod."

Keisha closed her eyes again and ran her fingers along the cool surface of the device. "I'm seeing . . . his eyes are closed."

Marcia said, "What do you mean, closed? Like, sleeping? You see him sleeping? Lying down?"

"I don't know. I'm just seeing him . . . I'm sure this doesn't mean anything."

"No, what is it?" Marcia asked. Pretty interested for someone so cynical.

"I don't know whether he's sleeping, or if it's something else."

"Like what? Are you saying he's—are you saying he's not alive?"

"No, I'm not saying that. I'm sure he's alive. But his eyes are closed, and I'm wondering if he might be unconscious."

"But you really don't know," Marcia said impatiently. "Don't get me all upset if you don't know what it—"

"Here's one of his hats," Dwayne said, coming back into the room. It was a basic ball cap, blue with a green visor, and a Hartford Whalers logo on the front.

Marcia opened her fist and displayed the check for her husband. "What's this?"

"Justin endorsed it. His signature's on the back," Dwayne said defensively. "Keisha said she needed a sample of his handwriting. I didn't know what else to get. Kids today, they do all their writing on the computer."

"You wrote him a check for two hundred dollars behind my back?"

"Marcia, really, this isn't the time."

"Let me see that," Keisha said, and took the check from the woman's hand. She flipped it over and ran her index finger back and forth across Justin Wilcox's signature. Wilcox was the last name of Marcia Taggart's first husband, Justin's father. "Can I have this?"

Marcia snatched it back, and tore away all the sections of the check surrounding the endorsement, including the part on the front with the account number, then returned the shred of paper bearing the signature to Keisha. "I don't see any sense in giving you all my husband's banking information."

"Oh for the love of God," Dwayne said. "Why not insult the woman while she's trying to help us."

"It's all right," Keisha said with unoffended patience as she tucked the slip of paper into the pocket of her jacket.

Marcia, plowing through her opportunity to apologize, said, "You were seeing Justin with his eyes closed. What's that supposed to mean?"

Instead of answering, Keisha took the hat from Dwayne, stood up and started to walk around the room very slowly.

"What are you doing?" Marcia asked, but Keisha,

who seemed to have slipped into some kind of trance, did not respond.

"Just let her do her job," Dwayne said.

Keisha was saying something under her breath, mumbling. Marcia said, "What did you say?"

She held up a hand and continued wandering. Then she stopped abruptly, turned and looked at Marcia. "What does scarf, or scarfy, or something like that mean to you? Does that word make any sense?"

Marcia's mouth opened. "What? That doesn't mean anything. I have no idea what you're talking about."

Keisha made a show of mental struggle. "Could it be 'scar free?' Is that possible? I'm seeing some kind of office. With empty filing cabinets. But 'scar free,' that must be wrong. Does Justin have any scars? Let me see his picture again."

Dwayne had shown her a picture of his stepson moments after she'd arrived, a framed high school graduation shot. A thin boy, with a long, angular face. Dwayne was about to grab it off the mantel and show it to her again when Marcia said, "Oh my God. You said 'scar free?' Is that what you said? That does mean something."

Keisha stopped kneading the hat in her hands. "What?"

"It was a clinic," she said quietly.

"A clinic?"

"They did laser treatments, that kind of thing."

12

"What could that have to do with your son, Ms Taggart?"

Marcia had become flustered. "They rented from—I have some properties. Investment properties, business space I rent out. I rented office space to the Scar Free Clinic, out past the Post Mall."

Keisha said, "Well, I must have this wrong. Your son could hardly be hiding out in a clinic."

"No, but they went out of business. The office space is empty."

Dwayne's eyes lit up. He gave Keisha an approving look. "That's why you just saw the empty filing cabinets."

"Could Justin have got a key to that place?" Keisha asked.

"I suppose it's possible," Marcia said. "Just a minute."

She got off the couch and hurriedly left the room. Dwayne said, "She's got an office in the house where she keeps keys to her various rental properties. Do you think he could be there? Is that what you're getting? Is that the vision you're seeing?"

"Please," Keisha cautioned. "Don't get your hopes up. I get these little flashes, I see things, but this might not be the thing that—"

"They're gone!" Marcia screamed from another part of the house. "The keys are gone!"

"There's something else," Keisha said. "I keep seeing him with his eyes closed." She paused. "Maybe he's just sleeping."

★

13

The three of them went over in Dwayne's Range Rover. Marcia, rattled, sat in the passenger seat, squeezing her hands together. Dwayne hit the wipers to keep the windshield cleared of snow.

"Why's he sleeping?" Marcia kept asking. "What does that mean?"

"I don't know," Keisha said quietly from the backseat. "But I think we should hurry."

"Can't you go any faster?" Marcia said.

"The roads are slippery!" Dwayne said.

"It's four-wheel drive, for Christ's sake!"

The former offices of Scar Free were on the second floor of a four-story office building. The three of them ran into the lobby, and after waiting ten seconds for the elevator to show up, Marcia lost patience. She took off down a nearby hall, pushed open a door marked "Stairs" and scurried up the single flight.

As they exited onto the second floor, they faced a door to an accounting firm. "This way," Marcia said, turning left, running to the end of the hall and stopping at a frosted-glass door with "Scar Free Clinic" painted on it in black letters. Someone had Magic Markered "CLOSED" on a sheet of paper and taped it to the glass.

"I have no key, I have no key," Marcia said. "How am I supposed to get in?"

Dwayne tried the door, in the unlikely event it was unlocked. No luck. He puffed up his chest and said to the women, "Stand back."

Keisha said, "I could be wrong. He may not even be in there."

But Dwayne wasn't hearing her. He reared back, brought up his leg, and kicked in the glass with his heel. It crashed to the floor with the sound of a hundred cymbals. Seconds later, the accounting office door whipped open and a short, heavyset man in a white shirt and skinny black tie looked on with alarm.

"What the hell is—Marcia?"

"It's okay, Frank," she said.

She reached in through the broken door to turn the deadbolt. The door swept back some broken glass as she swung it into the room. Their shoes crunched on the shards as they entered.

"Justin?" Marcia called out.

There was no answer.

The place was as Keisha had so briefly described it. Empty. Shelves cleared, filing cabinets half open, nothing inside them. No generic landscape pictures or diplomas or anything else on the walls.

But on the floor, several discarded fast-food containers. A pizza box, a Big Mac container still smeared with special sauce. Several empty beer cans.

"Someone's been here," Dwayne said. "Someone's been *living* here."

There was a spacious foyer, then a short corridor that serviced four examining rooms. Marcia was moving that way, opening one door, then another, Dwayne and Keisha running to keep up with her.

When she opened the last door, she screamed. "Oh God!"

A second later, Keisha and Dwayne found her on her knees next to Justin, who was lying on the floor, dressed in a pair of jeans and a black T-shirt, feet bare. His shoes and socks were scattered alongside him, and a winter coat was rolled up and tucked under his head as a pillow.

The young man's eyes were closed.

An orangey opaque pill container lay on its side a foot away from his head. Dwayne bent over at the waist, one leg raised behind him, and snatched it off the floor.

"Marcia," he said. "Aren't these the sleeping pills you were on a year ago?"

"Justin!" she said. "Wake up!"

"It's full of pills," he said. "It doesn't look like he's taken any."

Justin stirred. "What, what's going on?"

Marcia pulled him into her arms. "Are you okay? Are you all right?"

Groggily, he said, "I'm okay. I'm sorry, I'm sorry, Mom. I'm so sorry."

Now Dwayne had seen something else on the floor. A sheet of paper, with something scribbled on it. He grabbed it, saw what was written on it, handed it to Keisha without saying a word.

It read: "I know I've been a huge pain, Mom. Maybe your life will be better now."

"My word," Keisha whispered. Dwayne shook his head, looked at the pill container in his hand.

"God, if we'd been a few minutes later . . ." he whispered back.

"Justin, listen to me," Marcia said. "Have you taken anything? Have you taken any pills?"

"No, no, I just . . . I just had some beers, that's all. I was going to take them later, maybe. I don't know. I don't know what I was going to do. I'm sorry if I scared you."

Marcia clung to him and began to sob as he patted her head. Before Dwayne knelt down next to his wife and wrapped his arms around her and his stepson, he said to Keisha, "I'll see that you get your money this afternoon."

Keisha Ceylon smiled modestly.

Justin weakly put his own arms around his mother and stepfather. His face was buried in his mother's neck, his eyes closed. But then they opened, and fixed on Keisha.

Justin winked at her.

And Keisha winked back.

TWO

Ellie Garfield had been dreaming that she was already dead. But then, just before the dream became a reality, she opened her eyes.

With what little energy she had, she tried to move, but she was secured, tied in somehow. She wearily lifted a bloody hand from her lap and touched her fingers to the strap that ran across her chest, felt its familiar texture, its smoothness. A seat belt.

She was in a car. She was sitting in the front seat of a car.

She looked around and realized it was her own car. But she wasn't behind the steering wheel. She was buckled into the passenger seat.

She blinked a couple of times, thinking there must be something wrong with her vision because she couldn't make anything out beyond the windshield. There was nothing out there. No road. No buildings. No street lights.

Then it dawned on her that it wasn't a problem with her eyes.

There really was nothing out there. Only stars.

She could see them twinkling in the sky. It was a beautiful evening, if she overlooked the part about how all the blood was draining from her body.

It was difficult to hold her head up, but with what

strength she still had, she looked around. As she took in the starkness, the strangeness of her surroundings, she wondered if she might actually be dead already. Maybe this was heaven. There was a peacefulness about it. Everything was so white. There was a sliver of moon in the cloudless sky that illuminated the landscape, which was dead flat and went for ever. It was, it occurred to her, more like a moonscape than a landscape.

Was the car parked on a snowy field? Off in the distance, she thought she could make out something. A dark, uneven border running straight across the top of the whiteness. Trees, maybe? The thick black line, it almost had the look of a . . . of a shoreline.

"What?" she whispered quietly to herself.

Slowly, she began to understand where she was. No—not *understand*. She was starting to *figure out* where she was, but she couldn't *understand* it.

She was on ice.

The car was sitting on a frozen pond. Or maybe a lake. And quite a ways out, as far as she could tell.

"No no no no no," she said to herself as she struggled to think. It was the first week of January. Winter had been slow to get going, and temperatures had only started to plunge a week or two ago, right after Christmas. While it might have been cold enough for the lake to start freezing, it certainly hadn't been cold long enough to make the ice thick enough to support a—

Crack.

She felt the front end of the car dip ever so slightly.

Probably no more than an inch. That would make sense. The car was heaviest at the front, where the engine was.

She had to get out. If the ice had managed to support something as heavy as a car, at least for this long, surely it would keep her up if she could get herself out. She could start walking, in whichever direction would get her to the closest shore.

If she could even walk.

She touched her hand to her belly. Everything was warm, and wet. How many times had she been stabbed? That was what had happened, right? She remembered seeing the knife, the light catching the blade, and then—

She'd been stabbed twice. Of that, she was pretty sure. She remembered looking down, watching in disbelief as the knife went into her the first time, then seeing it come back out, the blade crimson. But it was only out of her for a moment before it broke her skin and was driven in a second time.

After that, everything went black.

Dead.

Except she wasn't.

There must have been just a hint of a pulse that went unnoticed as she was put into the car and buckled in, then driven out here to the middle of this lake. Where, someone must have figured, the car would soon go through the ice and sink to the bottom.

A car with a body inside it, dumped in a lake close to shore, someone might discover that.

But a car with a body inside it that sank to the bottom out in the middle of a lake, what were the odds anyone would ever find *that*?

She had to find the strength within her. She had to get out of this car now, before it dropped through. Did she have her cell phone? If she could call for help, they could be looking for her out on the ice, she wouldn't have to walk all the way back to—

Crack.

The car lurched forward. The way it was leaning, her view through the windshield was snow-dusted ice instead of the shoreline. The moon was casting enough light for her to see the interior of the car. Where was her purse? She had to find her purse. She kept her cell phone in her purse.

There was no purse.

No way to call for help. No way to get someone to come and rescue her. Which made it even more critical that she get out of this car.

Now.

She reached around to her side, looking for the button to release the seat belt. She found it, pressed hard with her thumb. The combined lap and shoulder strap began to retract, catching briefly on her arm. She wriggled it out of the way and the belt receded into the pillar between the front and rear doors.

Crack.

She reached down for the door handle and pulled. The door opened only slightly. Enough for freezing cold water to rush in around her feet.

"No no," she whispered.

So cold. So very very cold.

As water began swirling in, the car tilted more, its trajectory becoming alarmingly apparent. With her hands placed on the dash, she braced herself as her world began angling down. She took her right hand off the dash and used it to push against the door, but she couldn't get it to open any further. The front part of the door, at the bottom, was jamming up against the ice.

"Please no."

The last crack she heard was the loudest, echoing across the lake like a clap of thunder.

The front end of the car plunged. More water rushed in. It was over her knees. Then up to her waist. The windshield went black.

In seconds, the water was up to her neck.

The intense pain, where the knife had pierced her twice, receded. Numbness spread throughout her body.

Everything became very black, and very cold, and then, in a strange way, very calm.

Her last thoughts were of her daughter, and of the grandchild she would never see.

"Melissa," she whispered.

And then the car was gone.

THREE

The thing was, Keisha usually worked alone.

Okay, sometimes she'd have her boyfriend Kirk on standby to take a phone call if necessary, to provide a testimonial to a skeptical prospective client. But other than that, she liked to run her own show. The way you maintained control was to handle all the details yourself.

Bringing someone else into the mix, particularly someone without much experience, was risky. But there hadn't been much money coming in lately, what with Kirk not back to work, Keisha's car needing all new tires—she'd been running on three bald ones for months—and Matthew having to have those couple of teeth pulled. Keisha didn't have the luxury of being picky these days, and besides, she figured Justin Wilcox had as much to lose as she did—maybe even more—by screwing up this con on his mother and stepfather.

She had to admit, the kid was good. He not only conceived the whole thing, but pulled off his part without a hitch. He'd heard about Keisha from one of his old high school English teachers, Terry Archer, who had been persuaded to tell the class some of the details of what had happened to his wife Cynthia, whose family had disappeared when she was only fourteen, and whose fate had been unknown for twenty-five years.

It was big news at the time, when they found out what had actually happened. The story even made CNN. Archer had told his students that an incident like that, it brought all sorts of people out of the woodwork, which led him to tell them about the Milford psychic who'd claimed to know what had happened to Cynthia's family. How she watched the news, hunted for people who were desperate for information about missing loved ones, then swooped in and offered to help bring them all together again. Once they'd coughed up a thousand bucks, of course.

Keisha certainly remembered Terry Archer. It would have been hard to forget him. She hadn't liked him one little bit, or the wife, either. Not during her first visit with the Archers, at the TV station, where they were going to do a story on Keisha's amazing vision, or her second visit, to the Archers' home, when they literally threw her out on her ass.

You try to help people. No good deed goes unpunished, her mother used to say.

Justin told her Archer's experience had stayed with him, even though it had been four years since he'd heard it. His new stepfather, Dwayne, was a total sucker for this stuff, it turned out. He believed some people really possessed this ability, to sense things that others could not. He even watched repeats of *Ghost Whisperer*, which drove his mother crazy. Marcia said she could probably get the dead to communicate with her too, if she wandered around all the time in low-cut halter dresses like Jennifer Love What's-her-face.

"There are some things," Dwayne had evidently told his wife, "that we aren't meant to understand."

Justin told Keisha that was about the time the idea started forming in his head. What really helped spur it along was that his mother had cut him off financially. She used to give him, right off the top, fifty dollars a week, no questions asked, but how far did that go, really? You couldn't even do one night on the town for fifty bucks. How were you supposed to buy your beer and your weed and maybe something a little stronger, and something to eat on top of that? He tried to tell his mother, without actually mentioning the beer and the weed, that fifty bucks might have been a year's salary when she was a little girl riding around in a rumble seat, but these days you couldn't even put half a tank of gas in the car for that.

Then get a job, Marcia told him.

So that was how she was going to play it.

For a while, he managed to wheedle a hundred here, a hundred there, out of her. One time, he said he was debating whether to go back to school, which brought a smile to his mother's face. He had dropped out of UConn after the first semester. Loved the partying, but found the going-to-classes thing very intrusive. He told her he'd gotten his head back on straight, and was thinking about enrolling in a business school in Manhattan. There were several he wanted to check out. It was time to learn something *practical*, not all this airy-fairy shit they taught at university. That was music to his mother's ears. So he needed train and cab fare, and he might need to stay over one night. She gave him four hundred. Just like that. He never got on the train, but he did attend a fabulous party in New Haven and passed out on a Yale buddy's floor. Another time, after telling his mother he'd decided against school, but was going to get a job instead, he said he needed new clothes for interviews. He pocketed the cash she gave him, but stole a few things from a Gap so he'd have proof of a shopping trip.

Marcia asked him to model his new tops for her. When he pulled them on, he realized everything he'd stolen was a small, and he needed a large because he was six feet tall. No problem, his mother said. She asked for the receipt. She'd exchange the items for the right size next time she was at the mall.

No big deal, he said. He'd do it.

But she insisted.

Lost the receipt, Justin said.

You didn't have to be Sherlock Holmes to figure out what he'd done. That was when she cut him off completely. Even the fifty bucks.

Zero cash flow.

He didn't have any qualms about lifting a few things from the Gap, but he wasn't about to start robbing banks. A little too risky. Justin needed a way to get money out of his mother and stepfather, because when you were ripping off your family, it wasn't like you were actually stealing.

But you had to be creative.

Which was when he found Keisha Ceylon online, got her number, and got in touch. Face to face, he made his pitch. It was pretty simple.

"I vanish. They bring you in. You find me. They pay you. We split it."

Keisha saw a hundred things wrong with the idea. "Suppose they don't want to hire me. I show up, they slam the door in my face."

"You're not going to call *them*. They'll call *you*. Or Dwayne—that's my mom's new husband—will. See, my mom, she's not going to be in a hurry to call the cops, 'cause she'll figure the reason I haven't come home is I've done something really bad, like stolen a DVD at Best Buy or broken a cop car window or bitten the head off a squirrel. If she calls the cops and they find me, I'll just be in even more trouble, and when I'm in trouble, that means more aggravation for her." He grinned. "But Dwayne, he's totally into the kind of shit you do, no offence intended."

Keisha said nothing.

Justin continued. "I'll plant the seed. Next time we're watching *Ghost Whisperer*. I'll tell him, hey, there's a lady right here in Milford, does this kind of thing all the time. I'll tell him about when my teacher was talking all about you."

"Terry Archer."

"Yeah."

"I don't exactly have an endorsement from him on my website." The truth was, all the endorsements on her website had been made up.

"I won't tell Dwayne that part. But I'll send him a link to the website, so when I vanish, he'll know just how to find you. Who knows, he might even call you *before* we do this thing. Because he says he hears from his dead mother every now and then. He's a pretty nice guy, but he is a bit of a whack job. Do you believe that stuff? That you can get in touch with the dead and talk to them?"

She knew there wasn't much point in bullshitting with this kid, but it was hard for her to admit outright that what she did was all a crock. "Well . . ."

He grinned. "Yeah, that's what I think, too. Anyway, when I disappear, Dwayne'll remember that link I sent him."

Keisha shook her head. "He might not take the bait. He might never call me."

"Okay, well, I think you're wrong there, but the worst thing that could happen is I have to come back and think of some *other* way to get money out of them. But if he goes for it, and he calls you, then you text me, tell me it's on. No, wait, there's records of that shit. I'll check in with you from pay phones."

She thought about it. "There's another problem."

"What's that?"

"There's not enough money in it. I usually charge people a thousand. This is a lot of trouble to go to split that much money."

Justin flashed her a pitying smile. "You aim too low. Dwayne, and my mom, they've both got money. They'd be insulted to be ripped off for only a thousand. You could charge them at least five."

If she went fifty-fifty with the kid, that was a fast twenty-five hundred, tax free, because this was definitely a cash-under-the-table kind of transaction. Not bad for what would be a day's work, when all was said and done. It was hard to say no to a job this straightforward, even if it did mean taking on a partner. And it wasn't like there were people going missing every day to whose families she could offer her special talents.

A girl had to make a living. If something didn't come along soon, she'd be back to cleaning houses, and she did not want to start dealing again with rich, bitchy, mid-cleanse Darien housewives who had coronaries when they came home and found a soggy Cheerio in the drain basket.

Maybe it was the recession, but Keisha'd been seeing fewer clients lately for many of the services she offered. She read palms, told fortunes, organized psychic reunions. She'd throw in a little astrology if that was what floated their boat. The thing was, as long as you had a good imagination, there really was nothing to it. All you had to do was make it up.

Years ago, Keisha cleaned for a woman—not one of those Darien housewife types, but a nice lady—who'd once worked on the copy desk of a newspaper out west. Three weeks of their syndicated astrology column went missing in the mail so she cranked it out herself, off the top of her head. "Take the second bus, not the first. A good day for investing in friendship. A simple act of kindness will reap great rewards." How hard was it, really? The paper even got a few phone calls, that the horoscopes of late had been really dead-on, good stuff. Keisha figured if this lady could do it, what was to stop her?

At least Keisha had a few regulars, like Penny, the eighty-two-year-old totally batshit lady she went to visit every week so the old woman could talk to the child she aborted when she was seventeen. Handed over a hundred bucks every time because Keisha told her just what she wanted to hear: "Your unborn child forgives you, she's even grateful. This is not a world she wanted to be brought up in."

And there was Chad, the gay guy who ran a health-food store in Bridgeport and wanted his palm read whenever he was about to start a new relationship, which was often. Or Gail, one of her most needy, and well-heeled, clients, who believed she was, in an earlier life, either an Egyptian queen, Abraham Lincoln's wife Mary Todd, or Joan of Arc. She managed at least a visit every two weeks, and would have been in even more often if husband Jerry hadn't been clamping down on her nutbar spending.

Still, it was all barely enough to pay the bills, especially when her live-in boyfriend Kirk wasn't able to do much work since he dropped a cinder block on his foot five months ago when he had that part-time job with Garber Contracting. The foot was close to healed. Kirk wasn't limping all that much now except when he wanted to get out of doing something, like taking out the trash, or shoveling the driveway when there was enough snow that Keisha was probably going to get stuck.

He hadn't always been this way.

Okay, she had to admit, he'd never been a genius. He wasn't the sharpest tooth in the rotary saw. He didn't get a lot of jokes, unless they involved boobs, and once asked how they got the bones out of boneless chicken wings. But Kirk seemed like a good guy when she met him thirteen months ago. She was coming out of Penny's house after telling her that her aborted child, had she lived and grown to adulthood, would have ended up in a very unhappy marriage, and saw that her front right tire was flat. She'd never had a flat tire before. She'd had cars *stolen* before, but never a flat. Keisha didn't know if there was a spare in the trunk, and even if there was, she didn't have the first clue how to put it on. She stared at that tire the way she used to stare at formulas scribbled on the blackboard in high school chemistry class.

She didn't have money to call a tow truck. Well, she had Penny's hundred, but she needed that for groceries, and the rent, which was overdue. That was probably why she started to cry.

Across the street, a construction company was replacing a rotting porch on one of Milford's century-old homes. One of the workers cutting some boards for the decking noticed Keisha's plight, took his finger off the trigger of the saw, and strolled over.

Introduced himself as Kirk Nicholson.

Kirk looked in the trunk and found no spare. But there was a jack, which he used to get the flat off the car. He said his boss, a nice guy named Glen, would probably let him take his lunch break early. He'd take the flat over to the nearby Firestone store in his 2003 Ford F-150—how he kept it so immaculate when it was a working vehicle amazed Keisha—so she could get a new tire put on the rim. He knew a guy there, could give her a deal, wholesale price. Shouldn't take that long. Then he'd give her a lift back and put the tire on for her.

That's the way it happened.

While they were waiting at the Firestone store, Keisha learned that Kirk's mother, who raised him on her own, had died recently of a heart attack. He had no brothers or sisters. He told her about Glen, the man he was working for, whose wife Sheila had died in a bad car accident, and how he was raising their daughter on his own. Then he talked about his truck, that he'd got a great deal on it, he'd done a number of repairs on it himself, and was saving up to buy some high-end rims for it.

Keisha was more interested in learning whether he was seeing anyone. She asked him something really clever, like "Does your girlfriend like your truck?" At which point he said he wasn't seeing anybody right now. He was patient, and courteous, and never put a move on her once. When he was done putting the new tire on her car and had the jack stored back in the trunk, Keisha blurted out that he was welcome to come over for dinner.

That very night.

He said yeah, okay.

Kirk even seemed to like Matthew, nine at the time, who sat at the table with them while Keisha served spaghetti and meatballs. Gave the boy a ride in his truck, even let Matthew show how good he was at one of those Mario games. After the boy went to bed at ten, Keisha cracked two beers and she and Kirk sat on the couch and watched that show with Charlie Sheen, the one he was on before he went nuts and got fired.

"He falls asleep real fast," Keisha said. "And he's a *sound* sleeper."

Kirk wasn't so slow that he didn't understand what she was getting at. He started sleeping over that night. Within a month, he'd let his apartment go and had moved in with Keisha and Matthew.

It was perfect. At first. So nice to have a man around the house, reaching over and feeling someone in the bed next to you, bumping into each other in the kitchen, curling up on the couch to watch TV. Keisha kept waiting for him to hand her his share of the rent. She wasn't even expecting half. After all, she had Matthew. She was looking for just a third.

Finally, after he'd been there a month and a half, she worked up the nerve to ask.

"Work's kinda slow," he said. "Glen only needed me two days this week. And didn't I take us all out to Burger King Friday night? Even let the li'l fucker get a dessert."

It was the first time he'd ever referred to her son that way.

Keisha arrived home one day, four months after Kirk had moved in and still no contribution toward the rent, and there, in the living room, for God's sake, was a set of four mag wheels for his Ford F-150. "Winter's coming," he explained, "so there's no sense putting them on the truck now, and you don't have a garage, so they'll be okay here till spring. I'm gonna get a shelf from Ikea in New Haven, put them on display right there by the TV."

Not long after that, he injured his foot.

Even wearing safety boots, when the cinder block landed on his right foot it broke a couple of bones. Kirk had to quit work and keep his weight off it while he recovered. His biggest fault up to now had been how cheap he was, but these last few months he'd become increasingly, well, *mean*. Keisha didn't buy him enough beer, he complained. How could she have forgotten to buy him Oreos? How much had she made reading palms and telling fortunes this week, because he wanted his share? And the kid? Could he dial it down a bit? Always yelling and running around and waking me up when I'm trying to have a nap? And if he touches my wheels one more time, I swear to God—

Keisha, queen of the psychic con, had been flim-flammed. Bamboozled. The wool pulled over her eyes. Kirk had her thinking he was her dreamboat, but he turned out to be the anchor tied around her neck.

So, the bottom line was, Keisha needed money. If she couldn't get Kirk out of her house, she was going to need enough cash to move herself and Matthew out. Justin Wilcox's scam presented an opportunity she was willing to take, even though there was something about that kid that gave her the creeps.

"You sure you can pull this off?" she asked Justin.

"I took drama," he said. "Piece of cake. I got it all worked out. What I was thinking was, we pull this off, maybe we could do some other things together? I bet lots of times you need a backup person, am I right? Someone to help fool the customer? The mark? Isn't that what you call them?"

"This thing you want to pull on your parents, it's the kind of game you can only run once," Keisha warned him. "Once you've spent this money, you're going to have to find a new way to make more, and it's not going to involve me."

"Whatever," Justin said. "But let me ask you something."

"What?"

"All the other times when you go see people and tell them you have some vision about what's happened to a loved one, don't they get mad when you turn out to be wrong?"

"Who said I'm wrong?"

"Come on. It's just us."

"There's always something in what I tell my clients that connects in some way. I often tap into something that's very true."

"Except it's not something that actually helps them find who they're looking for," he countered, grinning.

"What I give everyone, for varying amounts of time, is hope," Keisha said defensively.

37

"Yeah, well," Justin grinned. "You know what'll be really good about this thing we're doing? This time, you'll be right. You're going to know exactly where I am. It's gonna look good on your resumé."

The job was behind her now.

It had been a week since Keisha had led Marcia and Dwayne Taggart to Justin's hiding spot in those deserted offices. Dwayne had, as she'd requested, paid her in cash later that day. She'd taken Justin's half, put it in a sandwich bag, put that bag of cash into a small Tupperware container, poured some spaghetti sauce around it, and tucked it into the freezer so Kirk wouldn't find it. He never made the meals, so she wasn't running any risk. As for her share, she'd lied to Kirk, telling him she'd only made a thousand on this job, half of which he demanded. The remaining two grand she'd hidden in a Tampax box that sat under the sink.

Justin had told her he probably wouldn't be around for a few days to collect. He knew his mother would want him to see "someone," and that she wouldn't be letting him out of her sight for a while. His stealing the sleeping pills, and that note he'd written her, had her scared to death he might hurt himself.

But sooner or later, he'd escape. He was planning to make a speedy recovery, psychologically speaking. He'd tell whatever shrink his mother lined up that it was just a blip, he was right as rain, it was all triggered by his troubled relationship with his mother (lay as much guilt on her as possible, he figured), but they'd patched things up, he couldn't be better, he was never going to do anything like that again, and while I'm here, have you got any samples of some fun meds I could take with me?

So when the doorbell rang that morning, seven days later, Keisha was not surprised to see Justin on her doorstep.

She'd been making Matthew's breakfast, the kitchen TV on, the volume down low. Kirk was sleeping in. Last time he'd been awakened too early, he'd come hobbling into the kitchen like a bear with its leg in a trap and thrown a glass up against the wall. He scared the hell out of Matthew.

So Keisha tried to keep things quiet this early, but at the same time, she liked to know what was going on in the world, so the TV was on.

"Hurry up," she said to Matthew, "or you're going to be late for school."

He picked at his breakfast, which was a piece of toast with peanut butter slathered all over it.

"Did you hear what I said?" she asked him.

"I'm not hungry," he said.

Keisha had noticed he'd been particularly mopey these last few days. Quiet, withdrawn, spending a lot of time in his room. She'd asked Kirk, "You got any idea why he's so down in the dumps?"

Kirk, dusting his mag wheel display in the living room, said, "Beats me what's wrong with the l'il fucker. He's just moody."

But Keisha thought it was something more than

that. Now, at breakfast, she said, "Somethin' on your mind?"

Matthew shook his head.

"Anything going on at school?"

"Everything's fine," he said. "Haven't I been good lately? Have I done anything wrong?"

She didn't have to think. "You've been good."

"So I don't see what the big deal is," he said.

"I was thinking," she said, "maybe after school today, we could go to the Post Mall, get you some new shoes." She could spare a little of that cash she had tucked away.

"I don't care about new shoes," Matthew said. "I just want to be able to stay here with you."

"You want to hang around the house after school today?"

"No, I mean, all I want is to be able to keep living here."

"What on earth are you talking about?" Keisha said. "You're losing your tiny mind."

"We never have a vacation," Matthew said. "We should go someplace. Just me and you. We could go visit your cousin in San Francisco."

"Yeah, well, Caroline may think the world of you, but she hasn't got much use for me," Keisha said. "You need to get moving. Go brush your teeth."

The boy took one last bite of toast and bolted from the kitchen. Keisha sighed and turned her eyes toward the television.

"We got off kind of easy with winter so far, not too cold,

but that's going to change starting tomorrow and continuing through the weekend as temperatures dip below freezing. And we've got a warning that even though it's getting colder, people should stay off ponds and small lakes, that the ice hasn't gotten all that thick yet and—"

The doorbell rang.

Keisha left the kitchen and walked to the front door. Standing there, one hand shoved in his pocket, the other texting on a phone, was Justin. His step-father, Dwayne, was parked at the curb in his Range Rover, engine running to keep the heater on. He waved.

"I told Dwayne I wanted to come by and say thank you," Justin said, ending his text conversation and devoting all his attention to Keisha.

"Come on in," Keisha said, and motioned for him to follow her into the kitchen. "And keep your voice down. My boyfriend's asleep."

Justin nodded, glanced around the living room as he stepped in, his eyes stopping briefly on the four oversized mag wheels on the rickety-looking shelves. He walked over to examine them, ran his finger over one, checking for dust and finding none. The shelf wobbled slightly.

"We have books on our shelves," he said.

Keisha said, "Come on into the kitchen."

"Police are investigating two liquor store robberies in Bridgeport last night. For a report, let's go to . . ."

"So," she asked, "how's it going?"

"Good," he said, nodding. "Like I figured, they

got me seeing a shrink. Mom wants me to see her a couple of times a week for like a month. But I can ride that out. Great thing is, Mom's being so nice to me. Buying me stuff, some video games, DVDs. I just got the whole original *Star Trek* on Blu-ray." He nodded and smiled, impressed with himself. "Things are good. But she's still kinda tight with the cash."

Keisha swung open the freezer and took out the Tupperware box. "Here's your share."

"Huh?" he said, looking at the frozen container. "What's in here? Lasagna?"

She ran the tap until it was hot, took the lid off the container, and ran hot water on the bottom. The sauce came out in one solid chunk. Keisha kept it under the hot tap until the sauce melted away, revealing the sandwich bag stuffed with cash.

"Man, you're like a spy or something."

Keisha opened the bag, took out the cash and handed it to Justin.

"In other news, a Milford area woman who went missing Thursday night is still unaccounted for."

"Awesome," Justin said, pocketing it just as Matthew walked into the kitchen.

"Who are you?" he asked.

"I'm Justin," he said.

"How many apps you have on that?" the boy asked, seeing the phone in his hand.

"A whole bunch." He held the phone so the kid could see the screen. "I got lots of games."

"Take my picture," Matthew said. "My mom says she doesn't have any good pictures of me."

"Matthew, please, the man—"

"It's okay," Justin said. He opened the camera app, took a shot of Matthew. Then he asked Keisha for her email address and sent the picture to her, the phone making a barely audible "whoosh."

Keisha handed the boy a paper sack that held his lunch. Matthew threw on his coat, ignored his mother's pleas to zip it up or put on his mitts and hat, and went out the front door.

The kid gone, Justin said, "You remember what I was saying to you before? That we could try something else? You and me? I mean, we did good together, right? It was fun. I should have job-shadowed you on careers day back in high school."

"I told you, this is it with us," Keisha said. "You had a good idea, it paid off, and now we're done."

She didn't want anything else to do with him. Something was wrong with the wiring in his head.

"Yeah, well, okay."

On the television, a man, his arm around a young woman, was talking about his wife. How he wanted her to come home. That if anyone was watching, who knew anything at all about what had happened—

"So, anyway, thanks. I better go. I keep Dwayne waiting any longer—"

"Shh," Keisha said, watching the report. The words at the bottom of the screen read: *Wendell and Melissa Garfield: "Mom, come home."*

"Whoa," Justin said, watching the TV. "You got a prospect?"

"Don't keep your stepdad waiting," she said, and ushered him out.

By the time she got back to the kitchen, they'd moved on to the next story.

FOUR

Keisha Ceylon stared at the house and thought, maybe she did have a little bit of the gift. Because there were times when she thought she could tell, just by looking at a place, that there was hurt inside those walls. Even a house where the blinds had been lowered, and turned so no one could see inside.

She sat in the car with the motor running, the wheezy defrosters just barely keeping the windows clear. Keisha was sure her feelings about the house were not influenced by what she already knew. She told herself that if she'd been strolling through the neighborhood, and had merely glanced at this home, she'd have picked up something.

Despair. Anxiety, certainly. Maybe even fear.

She thought about what this man, this Mr. Garfield, must be going through. How was he dealing with it? Did he still have hope the police would find his wife? Was he starting to lose confidence in them? Had he had any to begin with? Was he at the point where he'd be open to considering other options? Would he be desperate enough to accept, and pay, for the very special service she could provide?

Keisha was confident her timing was right. The man had gone before the cameras the day before. He'd been all over the news this morning. That was evidence of desperation, going to the media. That surely meant the police weren't making progress. That was always the best time to move in. You didn't want to leave it too late. If you hesitated, the police might actually find a body, at which point no distressed relative was going to need Keisha Ceylon's visions for directions.

It was, as she'd told Justin, all about *hope*. You had to get to these people while they still had some. As long as they had hope, they were willing to try anything, throw their *money* at anything. This was especially true when all conventional methods— door-to-door canvasses, sniffer dogs, aerial patrols, Neighborhood Watch—had turned up zilch. That's when relatives were open to the unorthodox. Like a nice lady who showed up on their doorstep and said, "I have a gift, and I want to share it with you."

For a price, of course.

Today's missing person was Eleanor Garfield. She was, according to the news reports, white, forty-three, five foot three, about a hundred and fifty pounds, with short black hair and brown eyes.

Everyone called her Ellie.

She was last seen, according to her husband Wendell, on Thursday evening, around seven. She got in her car, a silver Nissan, with the intention of going to the grocery store to pick up the things they needed for the coming week. Ellie Garfield had a job in the administrative offices of the local board of education, and she didn't like to leave all her errands to the weekend. She wanted Saturday and Sunday to be without chores. And to her way of thinking, the weekend actually began Friday night.

So Thursday night was dedicated to errands.

That way, come Friday, she could have a long soak in a hot tub, according to everything Keisha had quickly read and seen online or on television. After her soak, she'd slip into her pajamas and pink robe and park herself in front of the television. It was mostly for background noise, because she rarely had her eyes on it. Her primary focus was her knitting.

Knitting had always been a hobby for her, though she hadn't been as devoted to it the last few years. But according to one newspaper backgrounder that had tried to capture the essence of the woman, Ellie had picked up the needles again when she learned she was going to become a grandmother. She had been making baby booties and socks and a couple of sweaters. "I'm knitting up a storm," she'd told one of her friends.

But this particular week, Ellie Garfield did not make it to Friday night.

Nor did she, by all accounts, make it to the store on Thursday. None of the grocery store staff, who knew Ellie Garfield by sight, if not by name, could remember her coming in that night. Nor was there any record that her credit card, which she preferred to cash (she collected points), had been used at that store or any other that evening. Nor had it been used since. Her car was not picked up on the surveillance cameras that kept watch over the grocery store lot.

From what Keisha could glean, the police didn't

know what to make of it. Had Ellie met with foul play? Did she start off intending to go to the grocery store but someone prevented her from getting there? Or was it possible she had vanished of her own accord? The news reports didn't pose all the questions running through Keisha's mind. Was the woman having an affair? Had she gone to meet a lover? Did she wake up that morning and decide she'd had enough of married life? Got in the car and just kept on going, not caring where she ended up?

She certainly wouldn't have been the first.

But the woman had no history of that kind of behavior. She'd never run off, not even for half a day. The marriage, from all appearances, was sound. And there was the matter of the grandchild. Ellie Garfield was about to have her first, and had already knitted the kid a full wardrobe. What woman disappears on the eve of something like that?

Police considered the theory that she was the victim of a carjacking gone horribly wrong. There'd been three incidents in the last year where a female driver stopped at a traffic light had been pulled from her vehicle. The perpetrator—believed to be the same man in all three cases—had then made off with the car. But none of the women, while shaken up, had been seriously hurt.

Maybe Ellie Garfield had run into the same man. But this time things had turned violent.

On Sunday, Wendell Garfield went before the cameras, his pregnant daughter at his side. The girl was crying too much to say anything, but Wendell held back his tears long enough to make his plea.

"I just want to say, honey, if you're watching, please, please come home. We love you and we miss you and we just want you back. And . . . and, if something has happened to . . . if someone has done something to you, then I make this appeal to whoever has done this . . . I'm asking you, please let us know what's happened to Ellie. Please let us know where she is, that she's okay . . . just tell us something . . . I . . . I . . ."

At that point he turned away from the camera, overcome.

Keisha almost shed a tear herself when she rewatched the clip on the TV station's website. It was time to make her move.

So that morning, about an hour after Justin had left, she looked up the address for the Garfield home, which she found set back from the street in a heavily wooded neighborhood just off the road that led up to Derby. The lots were large, and the houses spaced well apart, some not even within view of each other. Keisha wanted to see whether the place was surrounded with cop cars, marked or unmarked.

There was a decade-old Buick in the drive, dusted white from a light overnight snowfall. Nothing else. This looked like as good a time as any.

She'd done enough of these that she didn't have to think about strategy. In many ways, dealing with someone whose loved one was missing wasn't all that different from dealing with someone who wanted their fortune told. It was the people themselves who fed the vision. She'd start off vague, something like "I see a house . . . a white house with a fence out front . . ."

And then they'd say, "A white house? Wait, wait, didn't Aunt Gwen live in a white house?"

And someone else would say, "That's right, she did!"

And then, picking up the past tense, Keisha would say, "And this Aunt Gwen, I'm sensing . . . I'm sensing she's passed on."

And they'd say, "Oh my God, that's right, she has!"

The key was to listen, have them provide the clues. Give them something to latch onto. Let them lead where she thought they wanted her to go.

Keisha just hoped Wendell Garfield wasn't as closed-minded as that Terry Archer character, who wouldn't let Keisha help his wife Cynthia. The hell of it was, she'd actually got part of it right. Just before the Archers threw her out of their house, she'd told them their daughter would be in danger. In a car. Up someplace high.

Wasn't that exactly what happened?

Let it go, she told herself. It was years ago.

But Keisha had a better feeling about Wendell Garfield. And the circumstances were totally different. With the Archers, it was a twenty-five-year-old case. There was no real urgency. But Mrs. Garfield's disappearance was in its early stages. If she was in some kind of trouble, presumably there was still time to rescue her.

Before heading up here, Keisha had tiptoed into the bedroom to do some accessorizing. You needed a touch of eccentricity somewhere. People figured that if you could talk to the dead, or visualize the hiding places of people still alive, or see into other dimensions, you had to be a little off your rocker, right? It was *expected*. So she went with the earrings that looked like tiny green parrots.

"What's going on, babe?" Kirk said, his face half buried into his pillow.

"I've got a lead," Keisha told him. "I need you on standby in case they want a reference."

"Yeah, yeah, I know the drill," he said, never even opening his eyes.

Sitting out front of the Garfield house in her little Korean import a moment longer, she checked the rear-view mirror to be sure she didn't have any lipstick on her teeth. Got her head into the right space.

She was ready.

Time to go in and explain to the frantic husband that she could help him in his hour of need. She could be his *instrument* in determining what had happened to his wife.

Because Keisha had *seen* something. She'd had a *vision*. A vision that very possibly held the answer to why his wife of twenty-one years had been missing for four nights now.

A vision that she would be happy to share with him.

For the right price.

Keisha Ceylon took a deep breath, took one last look at her lipstick in the rear-view mirror, and opened the car door.

Showtime.

FIVE

"So, what are you telling me, that there's been nothing, nothing at all?" Wendell Garfield said into the phone. "I thought, I really thought someone . . . well, if you hear anything, anything at *all*, I expect to hear from somebody, goddamn it. Do you have any idea what we're going through, what my *daughter* is going through? You tell Detective Wedmore I called. I want to hear from her. I want to hear from her the moment she gets this message."

He slammed the phone down. He'd decided, when he got up that morning, that he was going to be all over the police today, call them every hour if he had to. It had been a full day since the news conference. Half a dozen stations had aired the story. There was a clip on YouTube. It had made that morning's papers. If anyone was going to call in with a tip, it would be now. Wendell needed the police to know just how impatient he was. How he was expecting some action on this.

He'd called demanding to speak to the lead detective, a woman named Rona Wedmore. But she was out, and Wendell was transferred to someone else who claimed to be more or less up to speed on the investigation, and what sort of response the news conference had produced. There had been half a dozen calls to the hotline the police had set up. None had been considered useful. At least one was from an outright lunatic—a woman who claimed to have seen an actress on an Italian soap opera who looked just like the picture of Ellie Garfield. Had the police checked to see whether the woman had run off to pursue an acting career?

After hanging up, Garfield decided to make himself some tea, thinking it would help calm him. He hadn't slept more than a few minutes overnight. He was trying to think, since Thursday, when this had all started, just how much sleep he'd had. Five, six hours maybe? His daughter Melissa had probably had a little more than that, if only because the pregnancy so exhausted her.

Garfield hadn't wanted Melissa to go before the cameras. He'd told the police he wasn't sure she could handle the stress. She was seven months pregnant, her mother was missing, and now they wanted her to be on the six o'clock news?

"I don't want to put her through that," he'd told the police.

But it was Melissa herself who'd insisted she appear alongside her father. "We'll do it together, Dad," she told him. "Everyone needs to know we want Mom to be found, that we want her to come home."

With some reluctance, he agreed, but only on the condition that he would do all the talking. Once the lights were on and the cameras in their faces, Melissa went to pieces. She managed only to splutter,

"Mommy, please come back to us" before she dissolved into tears and put her face into her father's chest. Even he wasn't able to say very much, just that they loved Ellie and wanted her back.

He could hear murmurs among the news people, all indistinct save for one: "Good stuff."

Leeches.

He took Melissa home with him, tried to get her to eat something. "It's going to be okay," he told her. "We're going to get through this. We will, I promise you. But you have to eat. You have to take care of yourself. You have to think about the baby. You're going to have this baby, and you're going to take care of it, and everything's going to be okay."

She sat there at the kitchen table, looking as though she would crumble. "Oh, Daddy . . ."

"Trust me," he said. "Everything will turn out fine."

"How can you say that?" Melissa asked, her eyes red from crying.

"Because it has to," he said.

Melissa spent the night at her parents' home, but around six in the morning she walked into her father's bedroom to say she wanted to go back to her apartment across town. Garfield was still under the covers, but he was awake, and had been all night. He was reluctant to let her out of his sight, but Melissa said she could handle it. She wasn't going to stay at her place. She'd return and stay overnight in the room she lived in before moving out. But she needed to pick up some things, clothes mostly, and wanted a moment or two by herself. Melissa shared the apartment with her friend Olivia, but Olivia was away right now, visiting her parents in Denver. She didn't know anything about Melissa's mother.

Garfield said, hesitantly, "You're not going to do anything I should be worried about, are you? I mean, your state of mind and all."

She said no.

So he drove his daughter back to her place. Parked out front of the apartment, which was actually the top floor of an old house with a separate entrance. "Why don't I just wait here while you grab a few things?" he said. "Then you can come back with me."

Melissa told him to drive home, that she would call him when she was ready for him to pick her up.

Even though she was only nineteen, Melissa had been living away from home for three years. She was willing to admit, on the eve of becoming twenty, that she had been a difficult teen. She'd been a handful even before that. She'd gotten drunk the first time when she was eleven, lost her virginity at thirteen, and was dumb enough to leave marijuana in her room where her mother would find it a year after that. She openly ignored the limits her parents tried to set. Curfews were for breaking. Groundings meant nothing when you could open a bedroom window.

When she was sixteen, she dropped out of school. Ellie and Wendell decided they could take no more. They gave her an ultimatum. Get an education and live by the rules of this house, or move out.

The second option appealed to her more.

Melissa found a place to live with a friend from school. Olivia, two years older, was also young to be living on her own, but when you had a father who liked to crawl under the covers with you at night and a mother who refused to see what was going on right in front of her, you only had so many choices. You could stay and put up with it, kill the bastard with a frying pan upside the head, or get the hell out. Olivia got out. But as difficult as her home life was, she did well at school, wasn't into drugs, and held down a part-time job at Pancake Castle. She introduced Melissa to the manager, who gave her a stint waiting tables three nights a week. It turned out that getting kicked out of her parents' house was the best thing that had ever happened to Melissa. She looked up to Olivia, who was becoming a role model. Melissa was getting her act together. Without her parents to catch her when she fell, she had to stop falling so much.

She started to become responsible. Who could have guessed?

Ellie and Wendell were cautiously optimistic. Once Melissa got her head screwed on right, they figured, she could go back and finish school. If she did well enough, she might have a chance at college, Ellie mused one evening. Maybe she'd even think about becoming a veterinarian. Remember, she'd say to her husband, how when she was little, she said one day she'd love to work with animals and—

"For God's sake, Ellie, let's not get ahead of ourselves," Wendell said.

Melissa would come over for dinner. Some of these get-togethers went better than others. One night, Melissa would tell them about how she was getting her life back on track, and her parents would nod and try to be encouraging. But another night, Ellie, anxious to see her daughter's rehabilitation move with more speed, would start pushing. She'd tell her daughter it was time—*now*—to stop being nothing more than a waitress and get back to school and make something of herself. Did Melissa have any idea just how embarrassing it was for her mother, an employee of the board of education, to have a daughter who was a dropout? Who hadn't even completed the eleventh grade? How long was she expected to wait to see her daughter get on a path where she would amount to something?

Then they'd start fighting and Melissa would storm out, but not before asking out loud how she'd managed to live in this house as long as she had without blowing her brains out.

It always took a few days for the dust to settle after a night like that.

Ellie and Wendell still kept their fingers crossed that Melissa, despite these occasional blowups, was growing up. She held on to her waitressing job. She was saving some money, mostly from tips. Fifty to sixty dollars a week, which was at least something. And one day, talking to her mother on the phone, she happened to mention that she'd been on a college website, looking at what qualifications you needed to enroll in the veterinary program.

Ellie was beside herself with joy when she told Wendell the news.

"Isn't it wonderful?" she asked. "She's growing up, that's what she's doing. She's growing up and thinking about the future."

What neither Ellie nor Wendell had counted on was that the immediate future would include a baby.

Melissa was already three months along when she broke the news to her parents. They did not, to say the least, take it well, but Wendell searched for a silver lining. Maybe this meant Melissa would get married. She was young to be a mother, but at least if she had a man in her life, a man who could look after her, wouldn't that take some of the pressure off Ellie and him?

The man's name was Lester Cody, and he was thirty years old. A Pancake Castle regular. Always ordered four frisbee-sized chocolate-chip pancakes with double syrup and a side of sausage, only 1,400 calories. (Melissa had ceased to be amazed at how many people liked to eat this stuff for dinner.) He was, not surprisingly, somewhat heftier than the average man, at two hundred and eighty, but there was encouraging news. He was a dentist. He drove a Lexus. He had his own clinic. He pulled down a hundred grand a year. And—best of all—he was not married.

Ellie felt herself coming unraveled. One day she'd tell Wendell their daughter was ruining her life, having a child so young, but the next she'd confess how excited she was at becoming a grandmother. "At my age, who'd believe I'm a granny?" she'd say. She'd have long discussions with her husband about whether it would be a boy or a girl, to which her husband would grumble, "One of those two, I suspect." Then the next day she'd ramble on about Lester Cody, how he was really too old for Melissa, though he had a good job and could provide for their girl and their grandchild. But then Melissa dropped the bombshell that she really didn't have any feelings for Lester, that he was nice enough and all, but she never imagined that she'd be married to a dentist. She'd met another man, who worked at the Cinnabon in the mall, and he was pretty cute, and not as fat as Lester, even though he could sneak as many frosted buns as he wanted. Ellie tried talking some sense into her daughter, telling her that if Lester Cody was interested in her, and could provide for her, then she'd be out of her mind not to invest in that relationship. Because, let's face it, even if she wanted to go to veterinary college, she was going to have to complete her high school first, and how long was *that* going to take? Lester could probably get her a part-time job at the dental clinic after the baby came, answering phones and booking appointments and taking X-rays.

Melissa would scream at her mother to stay out of her life. And the next day, she'd call her up, asking for a lift to the doctor's office for her ultrasound appointment.

In between all the hand-wringing and exorcising, Ellie Garfield resumed her knitting.

"This child is coming one way or another, and it's

going to need something to wear," she said, and she would hold up half a sleeve and ask her husband what he thought of it.

It was more than Wendell Garfield could stand. Most times, in fact.

All this tension between his wife and daughter, the relentless discussions Ellie wanted to have with him about what their girl was going to do with her life. All this talk about the baby. How would Melissa manage? Would she marry Lester? Would he provide for the child even if Melissa didn't want to share her life with him? Would Melissa keep her waitressing job at Pancake Castle after the baby was born?

Sometimes Ellie would do a one-eighty, and lash into Lester Cody as though he were in the house with them. "Thirty years old! Sleeping with a teenager! He took advantage of her, that's what he did."

The discussions. They never stopped.

Wendell Garfield wondered if it was all this that had driven him into the arms of Laci Harmon, or if it would have happened anyway.

SIX

They both worked at the Home Depot, Wendell in plumbing most days, unless they were short-handed in some other department, and Laci over in home lighting fixtures. They'd had coffee breaks together, talked about their families, the joys and—mostly—heartaches of raising kids. She had two boys aged fifteen and seventeen who did nothing but fight with one another. Laci confessed once, only half jokingly, that she wished they'd have one final no-holds-barred battle and kill each other.

Wendell laughed. He said he knew exactly how she felt.

He always found reasons to stroll through the lighting section.

Laci often seemed to be passing through the plumbing department.

It started with friendly teasing, then double entendres. When Laci wandered by, she'd narrow her eyes and say she needed help with her plumbing. When Garfield was over in light fixtures, he'd bump into Laci on purpose and say he wondered if she could help him keep his light switch in the up position.

All in fun, of course. Totally innocent. After all, they were both, from all indications, happily married. Wendell and Ellie had been together for twenty-one years. Laci and Trevor, an assistant bank manager in Bridgeport, had just celebrated their twenty-third anniversary. They'd caught the train into New York, checked into the Hyatt by Grand Central, and taken in *Priscilla Queen of the Desert*, which Trevor, to his amazement, absolutely loved, even though he was not what you'd call a big fan of the drag queen community. It would have been a perfect getaway, except for when Laci took a beer from the minibar, and Trevor had a fit, telling her they could have gone to the closest grocery store and bought a six-pack for what that one beer was going to cost them. He wasn't going to mention it when they checked out, see if they figured it out later and charged it to his Visa.

Which they did.

One day at work Wendell had been asked to assemble, for display purposes, a vinyl-sided utility shed. He was inside the nearly finished structure, tightening up some bolts to make sure the thing wouldn't fall down in the wind, when Laci Harmon stepped inside, slid the door shut behind her, and placed his right hand on her left breast.

"Feel my nipple," she whispered. "Feel how hard it is."

Wendell had been touching the same two nipples for all of those last twenty-one years, although not quite as often as he once did, so feeling an unfamiliar one, even through Laci's blouse, was an electrifying experience. He thought he'd explode right then, and probably would have if he hadn't received a call on

64

his employee radio that someone needed help picking out a leaf blower.

They agreed to rendezvous that night at a Day's Inn. It was a Thursday, which meant Ellie would be out doing the weekly shopping, and Wendell wouldn't have to make some excuse about why he was leaving the house. But they'd have to be quick. Ellie was never gone more than two hours.

Turned out all they really needed was about ninety seconds.

"You're just nervous," Laci told him. "You've never done anything like this before."

"Have you?" Wendell asked.

Laci was horrified by the question. "Of course not." She pointed out that she was not that kind of girl.

Except now she kind of was.

They managed to meet once or twice a week. Not always at the Day's Inn, because it was expensive to have to rent a room every time. Sometimes they did it in Laci's Honda minivan. One time, they tried it in the backseat of Wendell's Buick, but he concluded that you're not quite as limber in your forties as you were in your teens, so they opted for Laci's van, which had seats that folded right down into the floor.

Handy.

The first few times, Wendell felt consumed with guilt. But the more Ellie went on and on about their daughter, the more he told himself that he had been driven to this. It wasn't his fault. It was survival. It was the only way he could cope.

Maybe, once the baby was born, and things with Melissa had settled down, he'd end it with Laci.

That was what he told himself. There were times when he even believed it.

A few minutes after he'd finished talking with the police, the phone rang. He thought maybe it was Detective Wedmore calling, but when he saw the call display, he swore under his breath. What the hell was she doing, phoning him at home? Did the woman have no sense?

"Hello?"

"Oh, Wen, I just had to get in touch."

"Laci, this isn't a good time."

"But I can't stop thinking about you, about what you must be going through," she said. She wasn't whispering, which told Garfield that she was alone in her house.

"Where's Trevor and the boys?" he asked her.

"He took the boys to Schenectady for a long weekend to see his parents," Laci said. "They'll be back later today. I'm just heading out the door to work. Wendell, you have to talk to me."

"What do you want me to say?"

"Have they found out anything? Do the police know what happened? I watched it on TV. I watched it at six, and I watched it again at eleven. It was very moving. You were very good, if you know what I mean. You held it together really well. I think, if anyone knew anything, if they knew anything at all, they'd call if they saw that."

"I just got off the phone with the police," Garfield said. "They haven't received any good tips."

"I feel . . . I feel so . . . It's hard to explain," Laci said. "I feel sort of guilty, you know? Because of what we've been doing, behind her back."

"Those things don't have anything to do with each other."

"I'm sure that's true, but I keep thinking, what if someone finds out? What if someone finds out what's going on between us, and they think it has something to do with what's happened to Ellie? And if, God forbid, something actually *did* happen to Ellie, then how is it going to look if—"

"Laci, please, don't go there," he said. "Maybe she just decided to go away for a while, clear her head."

"Is that what you think?"

"I don't know what to think. But I suppose it's a possibility. I mean, they haven't found her car or anything. If something had happened to her around here, you'd think they'd have at least found her car."

"So you think she just decided to drive away? Like, to Florida or something?"

"Laci, I don't know, *okay*? I don't have any god-damn idea."

His tone stopped Laci for a second. "You don't have to get angry with me."

"I'm going through a lot right now. I'm just trying to keep it together."

"How's Melissa coping?"

"Not well."

"What about that man who got her pregnant? Is

he still in the picture? Can he be there for Melissa at a time like this?"

"She says she doesn't want anything to do with him. Honestly, I don't think it would make things any easier for me if he was around right now."

"I was just—oh my God, I just thought of something," she said.

"What?"

"They're not tapping your phone, are they? They're not listening in?"

He felt a chill run down his spine. Could they be? He could kick himself. It hadn't even occurred to him until she mentioned it. He'd been doing such a good job, being the distraught husband, he hadn't thought there was any reason for the police to be bugging his phone. Sure, he knew the cops would probably be looking at him sooner or later, but he didn't believe he'd given any indication that he was in any way responsible for his wife's disappearance.

"I mean, if they hear us, and know we've been seeing each other, then—"

"Hang up, Laci," he said.

"—then they might think that you had something to do with it, you know, so that you could spend your life with me and—"

He slammed down the phone. If the police had been listening, the damage was done. They'd know he'd been having an affair. They'd know he and Laci had been seeing each other for weeks now.

Not good, not good at all.

Laci's call left Garfield rattled. He tried to tell

himself he was going to get through this. He had to keep his wits about him. Even if the police found out he'd been sleeping with Laci, it didn't have to mean he'd had anything to do with this business about his wife.

They hadn't found a body. Or her car.

And he was as sure as he could be that they never would.

Pull yourself together, he told himself.

The doorbell rang.

Jesus, he thought. They really *were* listening to his phone, and now they wanted to question him about Laci, about whether he'd killed his wife to be with this other woman.

He took a couple of deep breaths, composed himself, and strode through the living room to the front door. He pulled the curtain back first, to see who it was.

It was a woman.

A woman with green parrot earrings.

SEVEN

Keisha Ceylon was ready with her "I feel your pain" smile. First impressions were everything. You had to come across as sincere, so you couldn't overdo the smile. It had to be held back. You didn't want to show any teeth. No empty-headed Stepford Wife/ Jehovah's Witness smile that looked like it had been pasted on. You had to get into the moment. You had to *believe* you were on a mission. And you had to look as though you were sorry to even be here, that if there was anywhere else on this earth you could be, you would.

But you were *compelled* to be here. You simply had no choice.

She saw the man pull back the curtain to get a look at her, and gave him the smile. Almost apologetic.

Then the door opened.

"Yes?" he said.

"Mr. Garfield?"

"You a reporter? We did the press conference yesterday. There's nothing else I have to say at this time." He leaned out of the door, looking past her down to the street, wondering, maybe, if a news van was nearby.

"I'm not a reporter, Mr. Garfield."

"What do you want, then?"

"Let me give you my card," she said, handing one to him.

He glanced down at it. The card read:

KEISHA CEYLON
Psychic Finder of Lost Souls

Under that, a web address and a phone number. "What the hell is this?" he asked.

"Like it says there, I'm Keisha, and I'm so very sorry to trouble you at such a time. But I think, if you'll be kind enough to give me a moment, you won't regret my knocking on your door."

He looked at the card again. "Psychic finder. Sounds like total bullshit to me."

Keisha smiled. Not too much. Made the smile look just a little sad. "I encounter that a lot. Maybe it would be better if I just put the word 'consultant' on there, but that would be a misrepresentation of the type of service I provide."

"A consultant," he said, slipping her card into his shirt pocket.

"I consult for people who find themselves in situations such as yours, Mr. Garfield."

"So you're what, some kind of psychic detective? Like that *Medium* woman on TV?"

"Actually, a bit, yes."

"You have a nice day, Miss Cylon."

"That's Ceylon," she said, and put a palm on the door as he started closing it. "Let me ask you one thing before you send me away."

"What's that?" he said.

"Are things going so well in the search for your wife that you're willing to dismiss all other avenues?"

She could see the hesitation in his eyes. She said, "I'm not going to kid you, Mr. Garfield. What I do, it takes a leap of faith, I know that. And I'm not always right. It's not an exact science. But what if there's a chance, maybe just one chance in ten—a hundred, even—that I can help you find Mrs. Garfield, isn't that a chance worth taking? If it isn't, tell me, and I'll leave here and never trouble you again."

He held the door, frozen. It was wide enough that he could still see her, but not wide enough to allow her in.

After several seconds of hesitation, he opened it wider. "Fine, then."

She stepped into the house. There was a small foyer, and a living room to the right with a couch and a couple of soft armchairs. A set of windows along the front, the blinds letting in very little light, and a second, smaller window, on the side wall, where the blinds had not been closed tight.

"Do you mind if I sit down?" she asked. It was always a lot harder for them to throw you out when you were sitting down.

He pointed to an armchair. Before she could sit, she had to move a ball of green yarn with two blue, foot-long knitting needles speared through it. She tucked the bundle over to the edge of the chair.

"Have you ever heard of me?" she asked as he took a seat across from her on the couch.

"No," he said.

She nodded. "Well, it's not as though I'm famous or anything. But I do have something of a reputation. Just last week I helped a couple find their son. He'd been depressed and they were worried he might do harm to himself. We found him just in time, too."

"My wife was not depressed," Garfield said.

Keisha nodded. "Of course. Every case is different."

He eyed her as though she might already have had a chance to pocket the silverware. "Why don't you tell me what it is, exactly, that you do."

"As I said, I offer my services to people when they're in crisis. When they desperately need to find someone. Do you mind if I ask you a couple of questions first before I start getting into how I do what I do?"

"I suppose not."

"I saw you and your daughter—Melissa, is it?"

He nodded.

"I saw you on the news, making your appeal. Asking for information about Mrs. Garfield, asking her, if she was watching, to come home so you could stop worrying."

"That's right."

"I was wondering, what sort of tips have the police received since then? I'm assuming they've been in touch."

"There's been nothing. At least nothing helpful. A couple of nuts called in."

Keisha nodded sympathetically, as though this was about what she expected. "And aside from waiting for tips, what other efforts have the police been making to find Mrs. Garfield?"

"They've been trying to trace her movements since she left the house Thursday night. That's the night she does the grocery shopping, but she never got to the store."

"Yes, I knew that."

"And her credit cards haven't been used. I know they've been showing her picture around to all the places she usually goes, talking to her friends, talking to people she works with. All the things you might expect."

Another sympathetic nod. "But as with the tips, nothing very helpful. Is that what you're telling me, Mr. Garfield?"

"It would seem so," he said.

Keisha Ceylon paused for what she thought was a dramatically appropriate period of time, then said, "I believe I can help you where the police cannot."

"Is that right?"

"The police do what they do, but they are not trained to—what's the phrase?—think outside the box. What I offer is something more unconventional."

"I'm waiting."

She looked him in the eye. "I see things, Mr. Garfield."

His mouth opened, but he was briefly at a loss for words. Finally he said, "You see things."

"That's right, I see things. Let me make this as

simple and as straightforward as I can. Mr. Garfield. I have visions."

A small laugh erupted from him. "Visions?"

Keisha was very careful to maintain her cool. "Yes," she said simply. Draw him out. Make him ask the questions.

"What, uh, what kind of visions?"

"I've had this gift—if you can call it that, I'm not really sure—since I was a child, Mr. Garfield. I have visions of people in distress."

"Distress," he said quietly. "Really."

"Yes," she said again.

"And you've had a *vision* of my wife? In distress?"

She nodded solemnly. "Yes, I have."

"I see." A bemused smile crossed his lips. "And you've decided to share this vision with *me*, and not the police."

"As I'm sure you can understand, Mr. Garfield, the police are often not receptive to people with my talents. It's not just that they're skeptical. When I'm able to make progress where they have not, they feel it reflects badly on them. So I approach the principals involved directly."

"Of course you do," he said. "And how is it you get these visions? Do you have, like, a TV antenna built into your head or something?"

She smiled. "I wish I could answer your questions in a way that everyone would understand. Because if I knew how these visions come to me, I might be able to turn them off."

"So it's a curse as well as a blessing," he said.

76

Keisha ignored the sarcasm. "Yes, a bit like that. Let me tell you a story. One night, this would have been about three years ago, I was driving to the mall, just minding my own business, when this . . . image came into my head. All of a sudden I could barely see the road in front of me. It was as though my windshield had turned into a movie screen. And I saw this girl, she couldn't have been more than five or six, and she was in a bedroom, but it was not a little girl's bedroom. There were no dolls or playhouses or anything like that. The room was decorated with sports memorabilia. Trophies, posters of football players on the wall, a catcher's mitt on the desk, a baseball bat leaning against the wall in the corner. And this little girl, she was crying, saying she wanted to go home, pleading to someone to let her leave. And then there was a man's voice, and he was saying not yet, you can't go home yet, not until we get to know each other a little better."

She took a breath. Garfield was trying to look uninterested, but Keisha could tell she had him hooked.

"Well, I nearly ran off the road. I slammed on the brakes and pulled over to the shoulder. But by then, this vision, these images, had vanished, like smoke that had been blown away. But I knew what I'd seen. I'd seen a little girl in trouble, a little girl who was being held against her will.

"So, in this particular situation, because I did not know who the actual people involved were, I made a decision to go to the police. I called them and said,

77

'Are you working on a missing girl case? Perhaps something you haven't yet made a statement about?' Well, they were quite taken aback. They said they really couldn't give out that kind of information. And I said, 'Is the girl about six years old? And was she last seen wearing a shirt with a Sesame Street character on it?' Well, now I had their attention. They sent out a detective to talk to me, and he didn't believe in visions any more than I would imagine you do. Maybe they were thinking I might have actually had something to do with this girl's disappearance, because how else could I know those kinds of details? But I said to him, talk to the family, find out who they know who's really into sports, who's won lots of trophies, particularly football trophies, maybe even baseball, and the detective said, yeah, sure, we'll get right on that, like he was humoring me. But then he left, and he made some calls, and within the hour, the police had gone to the home of a neighbor who fit that description, and they rescued that little girl. They got to her just in time." Keisha paused. "Her name was Nina. And last week she celebrated her ninth birthday. Alive, and well."

Total bullshit.

Keisha clasped her hands together and rested them in her lap, never taking her eyes off Garfield.

"Would you like to call Nina's father?" she asked. "I could arrange that." She didn't think he'd take her up on the offer, but if he did, she had Kirk on standby. If Garfield called, Kirk would pretend to be the father of the little girl who'd disappeared. He'd say how they owed their girl's life to Keisha. He'd done this one other time for Keisha—not with a missing person case, just a woman who wanted a reference before she let Keisha read her palm—and he handled it okay. The trick was, keep the call short. Kirk was the kind of guy who couldn't keep track of the lies he'd told, and the more questions there were, the more likely he was going to trip himself up.

As Keisha had suspected, Garfield was not interested in confirming her story. "No, no, that's okay," he said. "But that's quite a tale."

Keisha detected sarcasm, but not as much as she might have expected.

"Still, I'd totally understand," she said, "if you'd like me to leave. Perhaps you've got me pegged as a con artist. There are plenty out there, believe me. If you don't want me to share my vision with you, I'll leave right now and you won't hear from me again. And I just want to say, I hope the police find your wife soon, Mr. Garfield, so that you and your daughter can get your lives back to normal."

She stood. Garfield was on his feet too, and when Keisha extended her hand, he took it. "Thank you for your time, and I'm so sorry to have troubled you."

"What will you do?" he said. "I mean, if you've had this so-called vision, and I'm not the kind of person who buys into that sort of thing, what will you do now?"

"I suppose," she said, "I'll go to the police with what I know, and see if there's anyone there who cares. Sometimes, though, that can have a negative effect. They're not always as receptive to my involvement as they were when I called them about Nina. I've found they have a tendency to get their back up, and the tip you give them is the last one they follow up." She smiled. "They can be somewhat dismissive of the skills I bring to the table. I hope, for your wife's sake, they don't take that attitude."

"So you *are* going to the police," he said, more to himself than to Keisha.

"Again, thank you for—"

"Sit down. You might as well tell me how this works."

EIGHT

What the hell was he to make of this woman?

Wendell Garfield didn't know what to think. Did Keisha Ceylon really have visions? Her telling of that story about the little girl was pretty convincing, but it wasn't enough to persuade him she was legit. There was something about her, though, that was hard to dismiss.

And worrisome.

His mind raced through the possibilities. The woman was trying to shake him down, plain and simple. He had a feeling that, even though they hadn't gotten around to the topic of money, it was just around the corner. What better mark than a husband desperate to find out what had happened to his missing wife? Wouldn't plenty of people in his position be willing to engage a psychic, a medium, a spiritualist, a paranormal expert—whatever the hell this woman wanted to call herself—even if they believed, at best, there was only a one in a million chance she really knew anything? Isn't that what someone who truly loved his wife would do?

Or maybe she wasn't trying to con him. Maybe she really believed she could do what she claimed. It was possible she was here out of a sincere wish to help. It didn't have to mean she actually had some psychic gift. She could be a well-intentioned nut. Deluded. Her visions could be the product of a twisted, disordered mind.

And then, of course, there was a third possibility: She was the real thing.

Garfield considered that the least likely prospect. But what if, somehow, for reasons he was not yet privy to, she was on to something? Did he want her talking to the police?

Not really.

The smartest course, for now, seemed to be to hear her out. See what she had to say.

Once Keisha was back in the chair, with Garfield sitting across from her, he said, "First of all, let me apologize if I was rude earlier."

"Not at all. I understand that what I do, the talent I have, is difficult for many people to get their heads around."

"Yeah, well, I have to admit, I have my doubts. But then again, I very much want to know what's happened to Ellie. I love her so much. This is just so unlike her, to disappear this way. Totally out of character. And it's been so hard on Melissa."

"Is she here?" Keisha asked.

"Not at the moment. She doesn't live here. She's been staying the last couple of nights, but went back to her own place this morning. I'm going to pick her up later."

"She's not very old to be living on her own," Keisha said.

"When Melissa was younger, she didn't care much

for observing our rules. So we all agreed it would be a good learning experience for her to try living on her own."

"I see," Keisha said. "And when I saw her on the news, it looked to me as though, that she might be—"

"Yes, she's pregnant."

Keisha forced a smile. "Isn't that wonderful."

Garfield couldn't stop himself from rolling his eyes. "Yeah, it's terrific. I don't really want to talk about Melissa. If you've got something to tell me about Ellie, if you've got some damn vision you want to share, then let's get to it."

"I get the feeling you're not going to be very receptive to anything I may have to tell you."

He shook his head. "Not at all. Go ahead."

"There is *another* matter we need to talk about first."

"Here we go."

"Excuse me?"

"I've been waiting for this. What's it going to cost me, to get a glimpse of this little vision of yours?"

Keisha adopted a look of great patience. "What do you do for a living, Mr. Garfield?"

"I work at Home Depot," he said.

"They provide you a salary for that?"

"Indeed they do."

"I bet you have to be very knowledgeable to work there. You have to know about so many things. About paint, and lumber, and plumbing and appliances. All the different kinds of screws and nuts and bolts? Am I right? They don't pay you just for the work you do. They pay you for what you *know*. For your *experience*."

"Go on."

"It's no different with me," Keisha explained. "This is my livelihood. I have a gift, and I'm offering to use it to help you. But I don't provide a service without some reward for my knowledge and experience. If you were to hire a private detective to assist you in locating your wife, you wouldn't expect him to put in his time and use his experience without compensation."

"Oh, of course not."

"I'm pleased to hear you say that."

"And what sort of money are we talking here, Ms Ceylon?" he asked.

"One thousand dollars," she said, not being the slightest bit shy about it.

His eyebrows went up. "You're not serious."

"I believe the sum is reasonable," Keisha said.

He thought about it. "I'm not a rich man."

"I understand," she said. "I've taken that into account."

"So there's a sliding scale? You take a look at the house and the kind of cars in the driveway, and if you see a Beemer you jack the price up? What the market will bear and all that?"

She started to get up once again. "I think I'll just be on my way, Mr. Garfield, if that's okay with—"

"How about this," he said. "You give me a hint of what your vision's all about, a little sneak peek, and if it sounds credible to me, then I'll give you five hundred dollars. And if the information you have leads to my finding Ellie, I'll pay you another five hundred."

She considered his words a moment, then said,

"I will tell you about a few of the initial flashes that have come to me. If you wish to hear more, how the images evolved, then I will tell you everything for the full amount of one thousand dollars."

He let out a long sigh, wondering how this all might look to a third party. His wife is missing, and he's going back and forth with this woman like he's buying a new Toyota. But he still didn't know what her game was, and he was wary, though it didn't strike him that he had anything to lose by accepting the deal she was proposing.

"Okay," he said.

"I'm very pleased," she said. "Not just because we've reached a satisfactory arrangement, but because I do very much want to help you."

"Yeah, yeah, fine."

"Do you have something of your wife's that I might be able to hold?"

"What for?"

"It helps."

"I thought you'd already had your vision. I don't get why you need something of Ellie's to hold onto."

"It's all part of the process. Some of the fuzzier details in my vision may come into sharper focus if I'm in possession of something that belongs to the person, something that's come into close contact with them."

"What do you need?"

"An article of clothing would be best."

"Like, her bathrobe or something?"

Keisha nodded. Garfield sighed, stood, and went upstairs. A moment later he was coming back down the stairs with a pink robe in his hands. It was faded and tattered from years of wear.

"Thank you," Keisha said, placing the robe in her lap and laying both hands on it. She ran her fingertips over the flannel material and closed her eyes.

Several seconds went by without her saying a word. Finally Garfield interrupted her trance state and said, "You getting bad reception there? You want to go outside or something? Get more bars for your vision?"

Keisha's eyes flashed open and she looked at him with something bordering on contempt. "Is it all a joke to you, Mr. Garfield? Your wife is gone, you have no idea whether something's happened to her, and you joke?"

"I'm sorry. Go ahead, do your thing."

She closed her eyes again, took a few seconds to get back into the mood. "I'm feeling some . . . tingling."

"Tingling?"

"It's a little bit like when the hairs go up on the back of your neck. That's when I know I'm starting to sense something."

"What? What are you sensing?"

Keisha opened her eyes. "This was what first came to me, when I started picking up something about Ellie's predicament. Your wife, she's . . ."

"She's what?"

"She's cold," Keisha said. "Your wife is very, very cold."

NINE

While Keisha was waiting to see whether he'd take the bait, thereby giving her a chance to reel him in, she was thinking about her starting point. Cast a wide net to begin with, then narrow the focus. Why not start with the weather?

It was winter, after all. *Everybody* was cold. Wherever Ellie Garfield was, it only stood to reason she'd be feeling chilled. Okay, maybe that wasn't true. The night she disappeared, she could have steered her car south and headed straight to Florida. She could have been there in a day, and by now might be working on a pretty decent tan.

"What do you mean, cold?" Garfield asked. For the first time since she'd gotten here, he seemed intrigued. Drawn in.

"Just what I said. She's very cold. Did she take a jacket with her when she left Thursday night?"

"A jacket? Of course she'd have taken a jacket. She wouldn't have left the house without a jacket. Not this time of year."

Keisha nodded. "I'm still picking up that she's cold. Not just, you know, a little bit cold. I mean chilled to the bone. Maybe it wasn't a warm enough coat. Or maybe . . . maybe she lost her coat?"

"I don't see how. All you have to do is look

87

outside and know you're going to need your coat. There's three inches of snow out there, for God's sake." He sank back into the couch, looking annoyed. "I don't see how this is very helpful."

"I can come back to it," she said. "Maybe, as I start picking up other things, the part about her being cold will take on more meaning."

"I thought you had a vision. Why don't you just tell me what the vision was instead of rubbing your hands all over my wife's robe?"

"Please, Mr. Garfield, it's not as though my vision is an episode of *Seinfeld* and I can just tell you what I watched. There are flashes, images. It's a little like dumping a shoebox full of snapshots onto a table. They're in a jumble, no particular order. What I'm trying to do, it's like sorting those pictures. Sitting here, now, in your wife's home, holding something that touched her, I can start assembling those images, like a jigsaw puzzle."

"You're pulling a fast one here. I think—"

"Melissa."

"What?"

"Something about Melissa."

"What about her?"

"There are these flashes, of your daughter. And she's crying. She's very upset."

"Of course she's upset. Her mother's missing."

"But even before. She's very troubled, Melissa is."

"I already told you as much. She's been a difficult kid. She moved out at sixteen, and now she's knocked up. She's troubled. Brilliant deduction."

88

"There's more," Keisha said.

Garfield leaned forward, placed his elbows on his knees. Really interested. Keisha liked what she was seeing. Another couple of tugs and the hook would be well set into that cheek of his. And all she'd really done so far was tell him things he already knew, things everyone knew. It was winter. He had a pregnant daughter. Her mother was missing. Who wouldn't be upset? In another minute or so she'd get to the next stunningly obvious thing—the car. But first, tease him with the daughter a little longer.

"What do you mean, more?"

"Something about the baby . . ."

"What about the baby?"

"Tell me about the father," Keisha said. Turning it around, letting him do some of the work, and feeding her a few more nuggets to work with at the same time.

"Lester Cody," Wendell Garfield said, shaking his head in frustration. "A dentist, makes more than twice what I do, drives a Lexus, a pretty damn good catch for Melissa if she'd only wake up and realize it. But guess what? She's not in *love* with him. Yeah, he's about seventy pounds overweight and'll probably have a heart attack before he's forty, but in the meantime, she could make a life with him." He pointed a finger at Keisha. "There's more to marriage than love. That's important in the beginning, but after a while, it's the daily stuff you have to get through. And Melissa's going to have a lot of that, raising a baby. She needs that man's support. Financial and emotional."

"And how does Ellie feel about all this?"

He blinked. "She, uh, she feels the same way. I mean, at first she was upset because he's so much older, but you balance everything out and Melissa could do a lot worse. Like that guy at the Cinnabon. Give me a break."

"Have Ellie and this Mr. Cody . . . has there been some kind of confrontation between the two of them? I'm seeing flashes, some arguments."

Flashes, yeah, that was good. Keisha knew that if she had a daughter who'd been knocked up and didn't want to marry the father, she'd be trying to talk some sense into her, unless the guy was a total asshole. But a dentist? What they made? What the hell was wrong with this girl? Keisha'd probably take the guy aside, give him some tips on how to win the girl over.

It was reasonable to assume Eleanor Garfield might feel the same way.

"She phoned Lester a couple of times," Garfield said. "The guy's pretty crushed about the whole thing. He really likes Melissa, and he seems ready to step up to the plate to support the child, but she doesn't want anything to do with him." He frowned. "Ellie was very upset about the whole situation. She talked about it all the time."

Was upset? *Talked*?

Move on, Keisha thought. The man's upset, not thinking clearly about his choice of words.

"Well," she said, "do you think Ellie might have gone to see Lester, to talk to him about the situation?"

But there *was* something funny about it, wasn't there? He'd talked about Melissa and Lester in the present tense. But when he mentioned Ellie, he'd slipped into the past tense.

Keisha was sure she hadn't imagined it. She wished she had the conversation recorded, that she could listen to it again. She supposed it could mean Garfield had already lost hope that his wife would be coming home alive. He'd already accepted the fact that she was dead. That was certainly a possibility, and if so, that was too bad, because *hope* was the essential ingredient. If the man had lost hope, he wasn't going to see the value in engaging Keisha. It had, after all, been nearly four days since he'd seen his wife. He could be forgiven for fearing the worst.

"Are you suggesting Lester may be involved in my wife's disappearance?" Garfield asked.

Now, there was an interesting thought. Maybe, at some level, Garfield harbored suspicions about the man. And Keisha liked that he was starting to ask her questions. Like he thought she might actually have answers. It would be easy to take him down this road, that maybe his wife had run into Lester and somehow they'd had an argument about Melissa, but Keisha thought it would be wiser to hold off on that, come back to it later if it seemed right. Maybe that's what Garfield was expecting her to do, to steer this discussion whatever way he led her. Maybe this was some kind of a test, so best to go off in another direction now.

Time to throw him a curveball.

"The car," she said.

"What?"

"I keep seeing something about the car."

"Which car? Lester's car?"

"No, your wife's car. A Nissan." She had read what kind it was online.

"That's right. A 2007. It's silver. What about the car?"

Keisha closed her eyes again. Took her hands off the robe that was still in her lap and rubbed her temples. "It's . . . the car's not on the road."

Garfield said nothing.

"It's definitely not on the road. It's . . . it's . . ."

Garfield seemed to be holding his breath. "It's what?" he asked, suddenly impatient. "If it's not on the road, then where the hell is it?"

Keisha took her fingers away from her head, opened her eyes, and looked the man squarely in the eye.

"I think that's as far as I can go right now, Mr. Garfield."

"What are you talking about? What's this about her car?"

"Mr. Garfield, I believe I'm closing in on something, and it's going to require all my powers of concentration. I don't want to be distracted, wondering whether you're going to do the right thing."

He ran his tongue around the inside of his mouth and over his teeth.

"The money," he said.

"Yes," Keisha said.

"I don't have a thousand dollars lying around the house."

"How much do you have?"

"Three hundred, maybe."

"I'll take a check for the balance," she said obligingly.

TEN

Garfield had to admit, when this so-called psychic talked about Ellie being so very cold, it scared the shit out of him.

When she hadn't gone into specifics, he figured it meant nothing. It was winter. It was cold. Big deal. Didn't mean the woman was frickin' Nostradamus. She had about as much skill communicating with the missing and the dead as that weather lady on the six o'clock news did predicting whether it was going to snow tomorrow.

But then she mentioned the car. Why had she suddenly wanted to talk about the car? And then she went and said it was "definitely not on the road."

She sure had that right.

That car was at the bottom of Fairfield Lake, forty miles north of here. No one was going to find it, not for a very long time, if ever. Water had to be forty, fifty feet deep there, he bet. It was probably already covered over with ice. It had gotten colder since Thursday night. It'd be spring before there was even a remote chance of anyone finding it. Someone would have to be diving, right there, to come across it. And even if some fishermen snagged on to it, it wasn't like the car was going to float to the surface like an old boot. They'd have to cut their line, put on a new hook.

How could Keisha Ceylon know the car was not on the road?

It could be a lucky guess. Simple as that. She could just be making the whole thing up. But what if she wasn't?

In that case, Garfield could imagine only two scenarios.

One, this woman actually had some kind of second sight. He'd never bought into that kind of thing, not like his older sister Gail, who believed it was very possible she was Nefertiti in an earlier life, bought all those books by Sylvia Browne—even got them on audio so she could hear them in the car—and claimed that at the moment their father died, he appeared before her to say how sorry he was he'd never told her he loved her. Gail's husband, Jerry, said she was snoring up a storm at the time, but so be it.

While Garfield was a skeptic, he was also willing to admit there might be forces at work out there he didn't fully understand. Maybe some people really did have special sensitivities and could pick up things everyone else missed. Maybe this woman did have visions. How else could you explain that story about Nina, the little girl kidnapped by the neighbor?

So if she had this gift, and really had had a vision about Ellie, then she knew something.

The other scenario—a no less comforting one—was that this psychic thing was an act. A total sham.

Complete and utter bullshit. A performance, to cover the fact that the information she had had come to her in a much less mystical way.

She had *seen* what happened. Not in a vision, but with her own eyes.

Garfield thought about that as he went into the kitchen for the three hundred in cash and his checkbook.

Suppose she had been there?

What if Keisha Ceylon had been at the lake that night? Maybe she lived in one of the cabins that lined the shore. On his way up there, Garfield had felt confident there wouldn't be any witnesses. That stretch of the lake was taken up mostly with seasonal properties. This time of year, most of the cabins were boarded up. By the end of November, most everyone had turned off the water, poured antifreeze into the pipes, put out the mousetraps, spread around the mothballs, covered over the windows, and headed back to their comfortable homes in the city, no plans to return until spring.

But Garfield now had to consider the possibility that one of the cabins had been occupied. Maybe someone—Keisha—had been looking out the window that night and noticed a car with its lights turned off being driven out onto the new ice with only a thin layer of snow on it. That sliver of moon was all the light anyone would need to get an idea of what was going on.

Someone could have seen that car creep out there and stop. Then seen a man get out of the driver's side with a broom in his hand, and watched as he attempted to sweep away the tire tracks as he made his way back to shore.

And then someone could have seen that same man stop and look back, waiting, *waiting* for the car to plunge through the thin ice.

Garfield shuddered at the memory. It had been agonizing. For a few moments there, standing out in the freezing cold, he was convinced the car was not going to drop through. That it would sit there, and still be there in the morning when the sun came up.

With his wife's dead body still strapped into the passenger seat.

He'd been talking, earlier in the day, to some customers at the Home Depot, a couple of fellows who lived up that way, who'd said the lake was starting to freeze over pretty quickly, that you could already walk out on it, but it wasn't thick enough to take any real weight yet. At least not for long.

He didn't think much about it at the time. But the conversation came back to him later that night.

After it had happened. After she was dead.

When he needed a plan.

Maybe Keisha Ceylon had been there, at the lake. Been that someone watching from one of those cabins. When the story about his wife hit the news, she put it all together.

And now she's here, shaking me down for money, he thought. Not quite blackmail. If she were that direct, if she were to say to him, "I saw what you did, and I'll go to the police with what I know unless you pay me," that would be taking quite a risk. For all she knew, he'd find a way to keep her quiet that didn't involve money.

He'd just kill her.

But using this whole psychic shtick, that was pure genius. She knew enough to get him curious, to get him worried. Worried enough that he'd pay her to find out just how much she really knew. Then, once she had his money, she'd keep things vague enough so he'd always be left wondering. She'd never have to tip her hand. She'd never have to let on that she was there. But she'd leave him knowing that if she wanted to, she could put him away for the rest of his life.

Well, Keisha Ceylon wasn't nearly as clever as she thought she was.

Wendell Garfield wasn't interested in taking any chances.

ELEVEN

After her father dropped her off and she went up to her apartment, Melissa felt woozy. And nauseated.

She'd only been inside the door a minute when she had to run into the bathroom. She dropped to her knees in front of the toilet. Made it just in time.

She cleaned up and found herself looking in the mirror. "You look like shit," she said. Her hair was dirty and stringy, and there were bags under eyes, not surprising, given how little sleep she'd had since Thursday night.

Melissa rested her hand on the top of her very pregnant belly, rubbed it, felt something move around beneath it. Then she felt her body begin to shake, her eyes moisten. All the crying she'd done in the last few days, she couldn't believe she had any more tears in her, but they just kept on coming.

She wanted to crawl into bed and never wake up. Just get under the covers, pull them up over her head, and stay that way for ever. She didn't want to ever have to face the world again.

It was all so terrible.

She couldn't stop thinking about her mother, about her father, about Lester, about the baby, about how her life had spiraled totally out of control in the last year. How it didn't look to her like it was going to get any better.

She thought about the press conference. About how strongly her father had felt she should not be a part of it.

"Don't do this," he'd told her. "Don't put yourself through it. It's not necessary. I can handle it."

"No, I should do it."

"Melissa, I'm telling you—"

"No, Dad, I have to do it. You can't stop me."

She recalled how he'd gripped her arm, how it almost hurt. How he'd looked into her eyes. "I'm telling you, it would be a mistake."

"If I don't do it," she'd said, "people will think I don't care."

And so, reluctantly, he had relented. But he was very firm with her. "Let me do the talking. I don't want you saying *anything*, you understand? You can cry all you want, but you're not going to say one damn thing."

So she hadn't. She wasn't sure she could have, anyway. Just as he'd guessed, she started bawling her eyes out. And those tears were the real deal. She hadn't been able to stop. She was so incredibly sad. And not just sad.

She was scared.

She knew her father loved her very much. She believed that in her heart. But it didn't give her comfort. Not now.

He'd told her what to say. He'd rehearsed it with her.

"Your mother went shopping and that's all we know," he'd said. "She went off like she always did. Anything could have happened. Maybe she ran off to be with another man, or—"

"Mom would never do that," Melissa had said, sniffing. She wondered if she'd put a little too much emphasis on the word "Mom," that maybe her father would pick something up in that. She'd seen him that one night, coming out of the Day's Inn with some woman, getting into the car together. But she'd never said a thing to him, never let on that she knew what he'd been up to.

If he'd noticed anything in her tone, he didn't show it. He was too preoccupied getting ready for the news conference. He kept drilling into her what her story was going to be when the police talked to her. Because the police were going to want to talk to her, she could be sure of that.

"—or maybe it's that guy who's been going around doing carjackings, maybe he did this. It could have been any number of things. The world is full of sick people. The police will have all sorts of theories, and if they never solve it, they never solve it."

"Okay."

"The main thing is, you just don't know. You have no idea. You were home by yourself that night. That's all you know. Are we clear on that?"

"Yes, Daddy."

She crawled into the bed, lay on her side, rested her head on the pillow. She grabbed a couple of tissues from the box on her bedside table and dabbed her eyes.

The phone rang.

She thought it might be her father, so she reached for the receiver without looking at the call display.

"Hello?"

"Oh my God, Mel? Is that you?" Her roommate, Olivia.

"It's me."

"I just got this message on Facebook about your mom, oh my God what's happened?"

"She's gone," Melissa said, and instantly realized it would have been better to have said she was missing.

"Gone where?" Olivia asked.

"Don't know. She went shopping Thursday night and we haven't seen her since. I was home by myself so I don't know anything about it."

Saying it just like her dad told her to.

"Like, what do they think happened?" Olivia persisted. "Did she have an accident? Did her car go down a hill or something and they haven't found it yet?"

"I don't know, okay? We just don't know. We're just, we just hope the police will find her."

"What can I do? What I can do for you? I feel awful I'm not there. How's your dad? How's he coping?"

Oh, he's fine, Melissa thought.

"I can't talk any more," she said. "I've got to go."

"Yeah, but what about—"

Melissa hung up.

"I can't do this," she said to herself.

If she couldn't handle a few questions from her roommate, how did she expect to hold up over the long term? How long could she keep this secret? How long could she hold back from telling what really happened?

What was it her mother used to tell her?

You have to live your life like someone's watching you all the time. Behave in a way that you can never be ashamed of.

She rolled over onto her other side, then back. It was so hard to get comfortable because of the baby. Finally she threw back the covers and put her feet on the floor, sat there on the edge of the bed with her head in her hands.

"I can't do this," she said again. "I have to do what's right. No matter who it hurts."

She wondered whether she should call a lawyer, but she didn't know any. She didn't want to pick one at random out of the phone book. Maybe she should call Lester. A dentist probably knew a lawyer. Didn't doctors and dentists get sued all the time? But then again, was there really any point? If her plan was to tell the truth, did she need anyone to represent her?

Melissa decided to take a shower first, make herself presentable. Before she stepped under the water, she phoned for a taxi. Asked for it to be out front in an hour. She stood under the water until there was no hot left.

She dressed slowly. Wanted to look nice. She didn't have all that many clothes that fit her these days, but she found something loose and billowy that would do the trick. She was standing on the curb when the yellow car came around the corner. When she got in, the driver asked where she'd like to go.

"The police station," she said.

"Okey-doke," he said, then laughed. "I was thinking maybe you were going to say the hospital."

"I got another couple of months to go," she said. "I'm not having a baby in your cab."

"Good to know," he said and put the vehicle in drive. "I've never had anyone drop a kid in my car, and if it never happens that's fine by me."

She didn't say anything the rest of the way. She was too busy thinking.

Thinking about how angry her father was going to be with her.

TWELVE

Garfield seemed to be taking his time in the kitchen, but when he returned, he had a stack of bills in his hand, as well as a check.

"Turns out I had four hundred and twenty in cash, so you can have that, and I made the check out for five hundred and eighty," he said, handing her all the paper. "I left the part where your name goes blank. I wasn't sure how to spell it. It is kind of a weird name you've got."

He'd evidently forgotten that her business card was in his shirt pocket, but that was okay, she could make the check out to herself later. She took a quick look to make sure it was okay otherwise. It was amazing how often people made a deliberate mistake so it couldn't go through. Got the date wrong, or didn't sign it. Keisha knew all the tricks. She'd tried them herself with her landlord. But the check looked fine. She fanned the bills to make sure the amount was right, slipped the check in with the bills, then tucked all the paper into a pouch in the lining of her purse, which she set back down next to her, open, on the carpet.

"Is everything all right?" she asked. "You were gone quite a while." She had wondered, at one point, whether he might have been calling the police.

"Fine, fine," he said. "I couldn't find a pen."

"You should have asked me. I have a couple in my purse here."

"I found one in the drawer."

"Well, shall we continue?"

"Would you like some coffee?" he asked.

"No, I'm fine, thank you."

"I was actually just about to make a cup of tea when you knocked on the door. Tea?"

"No, I'm good."

Garfield sat down on the couch. "So, do you live here? In Milford?"

What was going on? She'd brought Garfield right up to the edge of the cliff with that thing about his wife's car not being on the road. She had him then. He was curious, no doubt about it.

It was the ideal moment to hit him up for the money.

So off he'd gone to the kitchen to find the cash and cut her a check. And now he was back, ready to continue, and he was asking her if she wanted coffee? Tea? Asking her where she lived?

Was he stalling? Maybe he really had called the police while out of her sight, told them there was a crazy lady here, trying to exploit his situation. But wouldn't she have heard him if he'd done that? She could tell he was in the kitchen the whole time.

"I'm sorry, what was the question?" she asked.

"Do you live in Milford?"

"Yes, not far from here. Just before you cross the bridge into Stratford. We've lived there for a while."

"Children?"

"I have a son. He's ten."

"A son," he said, almost wistfully. "It would have been nice to have had a boy. Not that I'm sorry we had Melissa. But a boy, in addition to her, that would have been wonderful." He smiled. "So, Keisha, do you spend the whole year in town? Or do you have a summer place?"

Keisha thought this was getting very strange.

"I've just got the one place, Mr. Garfield, and I live in it all year long. Do you want to hear what I have to say, or not? I mean, you've paid me. I'm guessing you'd like your money's worth."

He gave her a go-ahead wave. "By all means."

"As I was saying, I've been seeing some kind of flashes of the car your wife was driving." Keisha still had her hands on the robe, occasionally kneading the fabric between her fingers. "The silver Nissan."

"You mentioned that the car wasn't on the road," Wendell Garfield said. "If it's not on the road, where do you see it?"

Keisha closed her eyes again. "It's not . . . a parking lot. I guess that would still count as being on the road, in a way. I'm not seeing it in a garage."

"What about water?" Garfield asked. "Do you see any water?"

Curious, Keisha thought. He'd just asked if she had a summer place, and now he'd mentioned water. She'd been thinking about Florida earlier. Maybe Garfield knew more than he was letting on. Maybe his wife had taken off for Miami with another man but he was too ashamed to admit it. Then again, she'd already put it out there that Ellie Garfield was very cold, so if she raised Florida as a possibility, she was going to get caught in a contradiction.

Stick with cold. So if it's cold, the water . . . could be frozen.

She closed her eyes a moment, then opened them. "It's funny you should mention water. I was seeing something, something shimmery, that I thought might be water, but I was thinking maybe it was actually ice."

"Ice," Garfield said.

This time, she kept her eyes open. "Yes, *ice*. Ice in a glass? Ice at a skating rink? Very flat ice? Maybe black ice, on the road, that caused the car to skid? Does ice of any kind have any significance to you? Any significance where you wife is concerned?"

"Why should it mean something to me?" he said, a defensive tone creeping into his voice.

"You were the one who mentioned water."

"And then you mentioned ice. I didn't mention ice."

"But it seems to have some meaning for you," Keisha said. "I could see it, in your expression."

"Why would you say flat ice? You mean, like on a lake?"

"That was just *one* of the kinds of ice I mentioned. But I can tell there seems to be a connection there. Why don't you tell me what that might be?"

Garfield stood up. He took a few steps to the right of the couch, then turned and paced in the other direction. He was stroking the end of his chin, pondering something.

"What is it?" Keisha asked.

He paced a few more seconds, then stopped. He looked at Keisha, studied her a moment, then pointed an accusing finger in her direction. "Maybe it's time you just leveled with me."

"Leveled with you about what?"

"About what's really going on here."

"I'm sorry, Mr. Garfield, but I'm not sure I understand."

"This whole psychic mumbo-jumbo act you've got going on, that's a load of bullshit, isn't it?"

Keisha sighed. "I told you, if you want to call Nina's father for a reference, I have no problem with that. I'm happy to give you the number."

"Have you got someone all set up to take the call? Someone who'll tell me what I want to hear?"

Keisha shook her head and gave him a bruised look. Trying to make him think her feelings were hurt. What she was actually thinking was, good thing he paid almost half in cash, and that she had the check. She'd hit his bank on the way home, get it cashed before he decided to call and stop payment on it.

"I'm very sorry you'd think that of me, Mr. Garfield. Just when I thought we were making some real progress here. I have much more to tell you."

"I'll just bet you do. And whatever you know, whatever you *think* you know, it's got nothing to do with visions or communicating with the dead or goddamn tea leaves for that matter. Whatever you know, you found out some other way."

"I assure you, I—"

"Give me my wife's robe. I don't want you touching it any more."

Keisha handed it to him. It certainly appeared she was done here.

"Thank you," he said, gathering it up into a ball.

Keisha reached down for her purse, set it into her lap, and started to stand.

Garfield said, "No, don't go yet."

"I can't see what possible point there would be in staying any longer, Mr. Garfield. I can tell that you view me as some kind of con artist. I've been at this long enough to know when my talents are being mocked. That's how some people react, that what I do is a sham, and if that's your conclusion, then I'm happy to be on my way." Thinking, *Don't ask for the check back, you son of a bitch. You'll have to dig into my purse to get it.*

"Did I offend you? Oh, I'm *very* sorry if I did that."

"You just accused me of having someone standing by to—to *lie* to you about my successes. Wouldn't you expect me to take offense at that?"

He was still pacing, still fondling the robe, doing something with it, like it was a mound of clay he was shaping into something. Keisha watched as he took a few steps one way, then the other. It struck her that this was how he formed his thoughts, by making these little journeys around the room.

"You *are* very clever, I have to give you that," he said.

Keisha said nothing. She was starting to get an inkling of what was going on. She should have caught on a little sooner.

"Very, very clever," he said, stepping over to one of the living room windows, peering through the slats of the blinds to get a look at the street. This put him off to one side and slightly behind Keisha, and she had to twist around in her chair to see him. "I'd like to apologize. Forget what I just said. Why don't you carry on, let me hear some more about your *vision*."

"Mr. Garfield, I'm not sure—"

"No, no, please, go on."

Keisha put her purse back down on the carpet and rested her hands by her thighs on the seat cushion. "Would you like me to start again with the ice, or move on to something else?"

"Why don't you just say whatever comes into your head."

Keisha had a bad feeling. She'd never dealt with anyone like this before. Garfield was all over the map. At one point, he'd lost interest in what she had to say, then wanted her to leave, and now he seemed to be having a change of heart, asking her to tell him more.

He didn't care what she had to say, but he didn't want her to leave.

Something was very wrong here. She thought she had it figured out.

It's him. He did it.

It explained everything. Keisha wanted to kick herself for not realizing it sooner. She'd been at this long enough, of course, to know that when a wife was murdered—or went missing—the husband was always a prime suspect. It wasn't very often people were killed by strangers. They were killed by people they knew. Wives were killed by husbands. Husbands were killed by wives.

The man had moved away from the window, and was taking a route behind Keisha's chair. She was going to have to turn around to keep her eye on him.

"On second thought, sure, tell me about the ice."

What threw her off was the televised news conference. She'd figured, first of all, that if the police strongly suspected that Garfield had offed his wife, they'd never have let him go before the cameras. Would they? She had to admit, he was good. Those tears looked real. The way he took his pregnant daughter into his arms to comfort her, that was pretty darn convincing, too.

Not that it had never occurred to Keisha that the people she preyed upon could be something other than innocent. Guilty people often made the best targets. They could be so eager to prove they were as much in the dark as everyone else that they leapt at the chance to pay to hear what she had to say.

Telling themselves, *I look so innocent. A real murderer would never pay a psychic for help, right?*

Maybe that explained why Garfield, at first, had agreed to listen to her. But something had happened during their conversation. The ground had shifted. He'd grown increasingly anxious. Had she actually hit on something? By accident?

Was it when she said his wife was cold? When she said something about the car being off the road? Had those comments been close enough to the truth to make Garfield think she actually knew what had happened?

It was time to bail. Maybe—and she couldn't believe she was even thinking of this—even give him back his money. Say something like, "You know what? Whatever vision I may have had, it's gone. I'm not picking up anything. The signals have faded. The flashes, they're over. So I think the best thing to do would be for me to return your money and I'll just be on my—"

But just then, a flash of pink before her eyes. Not a vision this time, though. It was the sash, from the robe.

And now Garfield was looping it around her neck and drawing it tight.

THIRTEEN

Milford police detective Rona Wedmore identified herself at the Home Depot customer service counter and explained that she was investigating the disappearance of Eleanor Garfield, wife of one of their employees.

"We wanted to talk to any of the people Mr. Garfield works with, and see if they can help us in any way," Rona said.

A short round woman in an orange apron said, "Oh yeah?"

"We're thinking, maybe Mrs. Garfield knows or is friends with some of her husband's co-workers."

"I don't think she really knows anyone who works here," the woman said. "I don't think I've ever met her, don't think I've even seen her in the store, although we all feel just terrible about what's happened, you know. We feel real bad for Wendell. What a horrible thing, you know?"

Rona looked at the woman's name tag. "You think you probably know Mr. Garfield as well as anyone around here, Sylvia?"

The woman shrugged. "I know him okay." She leaned across the counter so she wouldn't have to raise her voice. "But I guess, if you want the one who knows him best, you should probably talk to Laci."

"Laci?"

"Laci Harmon," Sylvia said, nodding knowingly.

"Are Ms Harmon and Mr. Garfield friends, Sylvia?"

"Well, I don't want to be sayin' nothin' that's going to cause anyone any trouble," Sylvia said.

"What do you mean by that?"

"Nothin', nothin' at all. I'm just sayin' that if you want to talk to someone who knows Wendell, you know, pretty intimately, she'd be the one to talk to." She put exactly the right emphasis on the word, hitting it not too hard, but just hard enough.

"I see," Detective Wedmore said. "Do you know if she's here now?"

"She is. You could probably find her over in 'lectrical or maybe lighting fixtures."

"Which way's that?"

Rona wandered in the direction Sylvia had pointed. She only found customers in the aisle displaying electrical parts, but there was a woman stocking shelves under an array of lit light fixtures. Wedmore could feel the collective heat of them overhead.

"Excuse me," she said. "Are you Laci Harmon?"

The woman turned with a start. Wedmore put her in her mid-forties, about a hundred and sixty pounds. Nicely round in the right places, and a little too round in the wrong ones. She had brown hair that hung straight down, wore no makeup, and looked at Wedmore through a pair of oversized black-rimmed glasses.

"Yes?"

Wedmore showed her ID. "I'm trying to find out what happened to Eleanor Garfield."

"Oh!" the woman said. "Ellie! It's a horrible thing."

"We're certainly hoping it's nothing too horrible," Wedmore said. "We're talking to everyone we can who might be able to help us, and I understand you and Mr. Garfield are co-workers."

Laci Harmon's neck flushed. "Well sure, we all work with Wendell. He has lots of co-workers. I'm certainly not the only one."

"I understand you might know him a little better than some of the others here."

"Who told you that?" Laci asked.

"Is that not true?"

Laci shrugged. "I mean, we talked, sure. You see someone at work every day, you say hello, you kid around, that kind of thing. No big deal."

"I didn't say that it was," Wedmore said. "You seem a bit nervous, Ms Harmon. Is everything okay?"

"I'm fine. Totally fine. I just, you know, don't get interrogated by the police every day."

"Does this feel like an interrogation to you? I'm just asking a couple of questions."

Laci Harmon laughed nervously. "I guess, you know, we're all a bit on edge, that's all. Worried about Wendell. You know, because of Ellie."

"Of course, I can understand that. Do you know Mrs. Garfield?"

Laci shook her head. "No, I don't. I may have met her once, at a staff thing a couple of years ago, but I wouldn't know her if I tripped over her." She put her hand to her mouth. "That didn't sound right. Like I would trip over her. Like she'd be lying on the ground or anything." A nervous laugh. "God, I'm sounding like some kind of idiot."

Wedmore didn't say anything, but was thinking the woman's name tag should read GUILTY.

"Like I said, I'm just so worried about her, hoping everything is okay."

"Why are you so worried about her if you don't really know her?"

"You don't have to know someone to be worried about them. I mean, when something happens to someone who's related to someone you care about, I don't think that's unusual or anything."

"You care about Wendell?" Wedmore asked.

"Okay, maybe that was a poor choice of words. I care about him the way I would care about anyone I work with, you know? That's all." There was a trickle of sweat running down her temple and she wiped it away. "It's so hot under all these lights."

Rona felt the same way, but said, "I feel fine." She could have offered to move this conversation someplace else, but decided this was turning out to be a very good spot. "How long have you known Mr. Garfield?"

"Well, let's see, I started here three years ago. I'd been working at Sears, but when they started advertising for jobs here I applied because it's closer to my house, and Wendell was already working here at the time, so I guess it would be three years. I've known him for three years. Yes, that would be right. Three years." She laughed.

"How has he seemed to you lately?"

"What do you mean?"

"Just what I said. How has he seemed? Has he been his usual self? Has he been acting as though he's been under more stress lately?"

"Of course he's going to be under stress. I mean, his wife is missing. Who wouldn't be stressed out by that?"

"So you've spoken to him since his wife disappeared?"

"Hmm?"

"I said, you've spoken to him since his wife disappeared?"

"Uh, let me think?" She ran her fingers over her chin in an exaggerated display of concentration.

"Ms Harmon, it's only been about three days. You have trouble recollecting things that recent?"

"No, no, I was just trying to remember when *exactly* I'd called him. You know, to tell him that we were all thinking about him here at the store, that if there was anything we could do, to let us know."

"And when *exactly* do you think that was?"

"I believe it was this morning," she said. She forced a smile and nodded at how successful her recollection had been. "Yes, in fact, it was this morning."

"Excellent," Detective Wedmore said. "And what did Mr. Garfield have to say?"

"Oh, just, you know, thank you for calling, it's been a very difficult time, blah blah blah." She was nodding so much she reminded Wedmore of one of those dog ornaments you used to see in the back windows of cars.

Rather than say anything, Wedmore folded her arms and looked at her.

"What?" Laci Harmon said.

Wedmore still said nothing.

"You already know all this, don't you?" Laci asked.

"Know what?"

"About the phone call."

"Why would you say that?"

"I knew it," she said. "I told him you might be doing it."

"What would that be, Ms Harmon?"

"Tapping his line. That's what you've done, isn't it? You've tapped his line. You're listening in on his phone calls. I know you can't admit it, I get that, but it just makes sense that you'd be doing it."

Wedmore thought carefully before she said, "When you told Mr. Garfield you thought the police might be tapping his line, why did you say that?"

"Oh God, so it *is* true? Oh God, no."

"Why do you think we would tap his line, Laci?"

"I swear to you, I had *nothing* to do with it."

"To do with what, Laci?"

"I mean, I don't know what he did with her. I don't even know if he *did* do anything with her. But if he did, you have to know, I had *nothing* to do with it. I would never get involved in anything like that. I have *children*."

Detective Wedmore nodded. "How long have you been having an affair with him?"

She put her hand on her forehead, rolled her eyes up in the direction of the hot lights. "Oh no, this is awful, this is—"

"Do you think Wendell Garfield did something with his wife?"

"I can't—oh, this is just—please don't tell my husband."

"He doesn't know about the affair?"

"He has no idea. Please, please—he's coming back later today from Schenectady with the kids. Please promise me you won't tell him anything about this."

"Ms Harmon, I'm afraid I can't make any—"

Wedmore's cell phone rang. She took it from her pocket, put it to her ear and said, "Wedmore."

"Kip here." Another detective.

"What's up?"

"The daughter in your missing mom case just walked in. Think she wants to tell you something."

FOURTEEN

Rona Wedmore found Melissa Garfield sitting in the interrogation room with Kip Jennings. Kip wasn't the lead detective on this case, so she was babysitting Melissa until Wedmore's arrival.

"Hey," Kip said when Rona entered. "We were just talking about kids."

Melissa's eyes glistened. She wasn't crying right now, but it was a safe bet she had been, at some point, since walking into the station.

"Hi, Melissa," Rona said. "How you doin'? I know that's a dumb question, considering what you're going through, but how are you holding up?"

"Not so great."

"Yeah, I'll bet."

"Melissa would like to talk to you about her dad," Kip said, getting out of the chair and stepping aside for her colleague.

"Sure, I can understand that," Rona said, taking a seat as Kip slipped out of the room. "He's going through a lot. He must be worried sick. Just like you."

Melissa nodded. "I want to tell you something."

"Okay."

"But before I tell you, I want you to promise me something."

"Promise you something about what?"

"About my dad."

"Well," Rona said, "it's kind of hard for me to promise you something before I know what it is you're asking."

"I want you to go easy on him."

"Go easy on him?"

Melissa nodded. "Because of, you know, whaddya call them? Extenuating circumstances. I mean, I know, my coming here, and telling you things, that it might get my dad in trouble, but I want you to promise that you'll take everything into consideration."

"That's what we do," Rona said. "We try to look at everything. But I can't promise you right now that there won't be consequences for things that your father might have done."

"I just hate getting him into trouble," Melissa said. "Even though I know that's probably what's going to happen."

"You know what I think, Melissa? I think you have to do what you know is right. I think you're carrying around a huge burden right now, and doing the right thing is going to go a long way to relieving that burden. That *is* why you're here, isn't it?"

"Sort of," Melissa said. "You know what? I know I only just sat down, but I really have to pee. What with the baby and everything."

"Sure, okay," Rona said. "Let me show you where to go."

Melissa went to the bathroom and a couple of minutes later they were back sitting across from each other. Melissa had one hand on the table and the other on her belly.

"I really love my dad," she said. "I really do."

"Of course. And I bet you love your mom, too."

Melissa looked down.

"Melissa," Detective Wedmore said gently. "Can you tell me . . . is your mother still alive?"

Melissa mumbled something so softly Rona couldn't hear what she'd said. "What was that?"

"No."

"No, she's not alive?"

"That's right. Dad's going to be really mad at me for telling you this."

"We can make sure he doesn't hurt you."

"He wouldn't hurt me, but he's going to be super pissed."

"I can certainly understand that," Rona said. "But I'm guessing you want to do right by your mother."

"Yeah, I've kind of been thinking that, too."

"Why don't we start with you telling me where your mother is."

"She's in the car."

The detective nodded. "This would be your mother's car. The Nissan."

"That's right."

"And where's the car, Melissa?"

"It's at the bottom of the lake."

The detective nodded again. "Okay. What lake would that be?"

"I don't know the name of it, but I think I could show you how to get there. It's about an hour's drive,

I guess. Although, even if I take you there, I don't know where *exactly* it is in the lake. And the ice has probably already frozen over. It's been cold. I just know she's in the lake. In the car."

"Okay, that's not a problem. We have divers for that kind of thing."

Melissa looked surprised. "They can go in the water even when it's super cold? And when there's ice?"

"Oh yeah, they've got these special wetsuits that help keep them warm."

"I couldn't do that. Swim in freezing cold water. I can't even go in a pool unless it's like eighty-five or ninety."

Wedmore gave her a warm smile. "I'm like that, too. It's got to be soup before I'll get in. So, Melissa, your father, he put the car in the water?"

"Yep. He drove out onto the lake, where the ice was thin. Then he waited for the car to go through." She started to tear up. "And then it did."

"How do you know this, Melissa? Did your father tell you what he did?"

"I saw it. I saw the car go through the ice."

"Where were you?"

"I was on the shore, watching." A solitary tear ran down her cheek. She bit her lip, trying to hold it together.

"Why were you there?"

"Dad needed a car to come back. I drove up behind him."

"So you saw all this?"

Melissa nodded.

"Melissa, do you know a woman named Laci Harmon?"

"I know who she is. She works at the Home Depot with my dad."

"Do you know whether they're close friends?"

Melissa cast her eyes down. "I think they've been having an affair."

"How long do you think that's been going on?"

"I don't know. I only saw them the one time."

"When was that?"

"Like, a month ago? I was driving past a hotel and I saw my dad's car and I saw her in the front seat with him. They were kind of making out a little."

"How did that make you feel?"

"Sad. And kind of . . . creepy."

"Did you tell your father you'd seen him with this woman?"

"No."

"What about your mother? Did you tell her?"

"No, I didn't tell her. I kept hoping maybe I was wrong, maybe I didn't see what I thought I saw, so I didn't want to say anything."

"Do you think that's why your father killed your mother? Because of this woman? That maybe he wanted to run away with her?"

Melissa blinked. "What?"

Wedmore repeated the question, and added, "It happens, you know. A man starts seeing another woman, his wife finds out about it, they have a fight, and then, well, you know. The wife ends up dead."

"Is *that* what you think happened?"

"It's one possibility. But maybe you know differently. Do you know why your father killed your mother?"

"Dad didn't kill her. Is that what you've been thinking?"

Now it was Wedmore's turn to look surprised.

"Isn't that why you're here, Melissa?"

The dead woman's daughter sighed and shook her head. "I guess I should start at the beginning."

FIFTEEN

When Keisha Ceylon saw the pink sash drop past her eyes, she reached up instinctively to get her fingers between it and her neck. But she wasn't quick enough. Wendell Garfield wrapped it tightly around her throat and began to twist.

"I swear, I don't know how you know, but you're not going to tell anyone," he said.

Keisha clawed at the sash, her fingernails ripping into her own skin as she tried to loosen his hold on her. But the satiny ribbon was already cutting deep into her neck and there wasn't a hope of getting her fingers in there.

Garfield was leaning down over her, his mouth close to her right ear. His breath was hot against her cheek.

She tried to say something, to scream, but with her windpipe squeezed, nothing came out. Not a sound. She felt her eyes bulging. She kicked at the floor, dug into the carpet with her heels.

Keisha Ceylon knew, in that instant, that she was going to die. She didn't need mystical skills for that vision of the future.

It certainly wasn't going to be the *distant* future.

A number of thoughts ran through her head during those milliseconds. One wouldn't have expected there to be much time for introspection, but the world has a way of slowing down during such moments, and Keisha had an opportunity to think: *Maybe I've had this coming.*

You go around making your living by exploiting people at their most vulnerable, wasn't there bound to be a reckoning at some point? If there was anyone who'd believe in karma, wouldn't it be Keisha?

Wouldn't English teacher Terry Archer love to see her now? Wouldn't her predicament make the perfect lesson the next time he was trying to get across to his students the concept of irony? Especially the part about how Keisha never saw it coming. How she walked right into it.

Pretty goddamn rich, she had to admit.

And yet, in that moment, she didn't feel bitter. What she felt was regretful. If she could have spoken, if she'd been able to get a breath of air, what she might have said was, "Sorry."

There were more than a few people who deserved an apology. But the person whose face floated before her eyes first was Matthew's.

"Sorry, sweetheart," she heard herself saying. "Sorry Mommy fucked up."

All these thoughts fired through her synapses in a fraction of a second. She might have liked to spend even more time considering how her misdeeds had impacted herself and others, to have done a bit of soul-searching, but there was a part of her brain that was deliberating over more immediate matters.

Even though things look pretty bad right now, I need to try to get out of this.

Which was why she was still clawing at her throat, trying, without success, to get her fingers under the bathrobe sash.

"You must have been there," Garfield said through gritted teeth. "You had to be watching. That's the only way I can figure it. You were up there, you saw me put the car on the ice, you saw it go under, and then you figured you could blackmail me. A thousand today, another thousand next week, and then the week after that, until I had nothing left."

He had the ends of the sash twisted several times around his palms and kept pulling. Keisha could feel herself starting to lose consciousness. Her fingers stopped trying. Her hands fell away from her neck and landed next to her, resting on the chair cushion. She wondered, ever so briefly, what he would do with her body. She hoped he wouldn't put her in the lake along with Mrs. Garfield.

She didn't like the water. When she was ten, her mother briefly dated a man who had a place on Cape Cod, and Keisha never so much as stuck her toe into the Atlantic. She had a fear of sharks from that movie. No way she was going out into that. Luckily, they never went back because the man decided to return to his wife.

In the seconds just before Keisha figured she was going to black out, her fingers dug into the seat of her chair.

Her right hand brushed up against something.

Something soft, almost furry.

Yarn.

And as her fingers fumbled across the yarn, they landed on something else. Something long, and narrow, and pointed. Like a stick, or a needle.

A knitting needle.

In the last second Keisha had before she blacked out, she grasped the knitting needle with her right hand and swung her hand up and over her shoulder. As hard as she could.

The scream was only an inch from her ear. And it was horrific.

As the grip on Keisha's neck slackened, she tumbled forward out of the chair and collapsed onto the floor, gasping for breath. She was on her knees, one hand on the floor supporting her, the other on her neck. Air rushed into her lungs so quickly it hurt. Her gasps would have been loud enough to hear from anywhere in the house, were it not for Wendell Garfield's anguished screams.

Keisha, even as she struggled to get her breath back, had to turn and see what she had done.

The knitting needle was sticking straight out of Garfield's right eye. Blood poured from the socket, covering the right half of his face. Judging by how much of the needle remained exposed, Keisha figured a good four to five inches of it was buried in his head.

But he could see her with his left eye, and, still

screaming, proceeded to come around the chair after her.

Keisha struggled to her feet, moving in the direction of the door. But she hit her knee going around the corner of the coffee table and stumbled, allowing Garfield to get close enough to clamp his hand onto her arm.

"You bitch!" Garfield said, although there was blood leaking into his throat and it sounded as though he was gargling.

He yanked so hard on her arm that Keisha went down to the floor again. She landed on her back, and before she had a chance to roll away, he was on top of her, straddling her mid-section.

He didn't have the sash any more. He was going to finish her off with his bare hands. He leaned forward, the knitting needle still sticking out of his eye socket, blood dripping—no, pouring—onto Keisha, and got his fingers and thumbs around her neck. She flailed about, but he had her neck pinned to the floor.

She started blacking out all over again. With her last ounce of strength she raised her hand and shot the heel of it straight up against the end of the knitting needle.

She drove the plastic spear another three inches into Garfield's head.

There was another scream, and then, for a moment, he froze above her. His grip on her neck relaxed, his arms went weak, and his body collapsed on top of her.

Keisha didn't even take time to get her breath back this time. She pushed frantically at his dead body until it was off of her, crawled a few feet away, and then, once she was able to breathe normally again, decided she had earned the right to take a moment and become hysterical.

SIXTEEN

"You're sure you don't want a lawyer?" Rona Wedmore asked.

"I'm positive," Melissa Garfield said. "I'm going to plead guilty to everything." Like a child saying she'd eaten all her vegetables.

"Then you have to sign here. And here."

Melissa scribbled her signature.

"Okay, then why don't you start from the beginning."

"You see," Melissa said, "instead of going shopping first, Mom decided to visit me. She'd do that once in a while, just drop by without calling or anything. She'd say, 'What, a mother can't pop in and visit her daughter?' She comes in and I'm in the kitchen, cutting up some celery and carrot sticks to put in a salad because I'm actually trying to eat the right things so the baby will be healthy, you know, even though I'd rather just be eating pizza and burgers, but I'm *trying*, okay? I'm really trying."

"Sure," Wedmore said.

"It's like she was checking up on me all the time. She was always asking me these questions, like what's happening with Lester and would I marry him and let him take care of us or was I going to move back in with her and Dad, like I really wanted to do that, right? And then she wanted to know if I'd gotten any more information about the veterinarian school I've been thinking about going to one day because I like animals, like especially dogs and cats."

"I like dogs and cats, too," Wedmore said.

"Yeah. And so she was asking me about that and I said not yet, but I was thinking about it and she said what's the holdup? Why don't I see if I could register now, even though that makes no sense because I have to finish all my high school stuff first, you know, and she knows all that, right? But she's saying if I applied early it would show them that I'm really interested and I said Jesus, will you just give me some room to breathe, you know? I got a baby coming in a few weeks and I got a lot on my mind and okay, maybe I'm thinking about my future, but do I have to do something about it right this very fucking second? And she said, it'll take you like two minutes so why don't you do it and I'll cut up your celery and your carrots and she says I'm not cutting them up small enough anyway and she tries to take the knife from me and I don't know what happened but I kind of snapped or something, you know?"

"Sure," Rona Wedmore said, nodding sympathetically.

"So, like, I don't know how exactly it happened, but the knife sort of went into her, and then I guess I must have put it into her a second time, and then she looks at me and she's all like, what have you done? And then she falls down and she doesn't move or anything."

"So what did you do then? Did you think about calling for an ambulance?"

"I guess I went all crazy for a while, you know? But I managed to call my dad."

"Okay."

"I said something's happened to Mom, you have to get over here, and he said, is it a heart attack or something, and I said no, and he said I should call 911, and then I said that I'd kind of stabbed her, and that she wasn't breathing or moving or anything and then he was all 'What?' And he said I shouldn't do anything and he'd be right over."

"To help you?"

Melissa nodded. "So he got over real soon, and he was kind of all freaked out, and he took one look at Mom and could see that she was dead, and he said he had to think. I asked him, was I going to go to jail? Was I going to have my baby in jail, and he kept telling me to shut up, that he was thinking, and then he had this idea. He got Mom out of the apartment the back way and into her car, and then he told me I was going to have to follow in his car, drive along after him. And I followed him up to this lake, and he put the car on the ice and it went through and I guess I already told you about that part."

"And then what happened?"

"Dad came back to my place and cleaned up. There was blood all over the place. It was horrible. It took hours to clean it all up. It's a good thing my roommate was away or she'd have seen everything that happened and that would have been bad. I couldn't help my dad with cleaning up. My head had really kind of exploded by this point, and I was super tired. All that had happened, and then having to drive up to the lake. I stayed in my bed, under the covers. When he was finished, he told me everything was going to be okay. He said I wasn't going to have to go to jail." She smiled sadly. "He said he loved me very much and he wanted everything to be okay for me. He said I'd done a bad thing but sometimes people made mistakes and he didn't want my whole life to be ruined, you know? He's a really good dad. He said the police would just think Mom ran away, or maybe she got killed by that carjacker guy, but they'd never really know what happened because they'd never be able to find Mom or her car. And if the police didn't know what happened, they couldn't really charge anyone."

She shook her head. "He's going to be so mad at me. Because he did all this to protect me, and now . . . well, here I am. But I just . . . I can't do it. I feel bad about what I did. I really loved my mom."

Wedmore reached out and touched her hand. "Of course you did."

"Is my dad going to be in a lot of trouble?"

"Well, I'd have to say yes. But with the right lawyer, and a sympathetic jury . . . A lot of them will understand the lengths a father might go to, to help his daughter. He might have to go to jail, but maybe not for a long term."

"Not as long as me."

Wedmore smiled. "You might be right about that."

Melissa even managed a smile herself. "You're very nice. I'm glad you were the one I got to tell all this to."

"Me too," the detective said.

"I just hope you're right, that they don't send Dad away to jail for a long time. That wouldn't be fair. He's not that old a guy. He's got a lot of time left."

SEVENTEEN

Keisha was not calling the police.

It didn't matter that what she'd done was in self-defense. This was no premeditated murder. Wendell Garfield had tried to kill her, and if she hadn't put that knitting needle into his brain, he'd have succeeded.

She knew that if she did go to the police, she might even be able to make a pretty good case for herself. She'd start by telling them that Garfield had murdered his wife. He'd put her body in a car and left it on a frozen lake and waited for it to drop through the ice. Then he'd tried to kill Keisha when she'd figured out what he'd done.

Well, sort of figured it out. She'd be the first to admit she'd got a bit lucky with the vision thing, although lucky didn't exactly seem like the right word in this instance.

And while she hadn't yet looked in a mirror, she knew from touching her neck that there were some very serious marks where Garfield had tightened that sash. If her story didn't entirely convince the police, surely those marks across her throat would.

So, maybe, if she went to the cops, they'd buy her story.

But why take the chance?

If she did come forward, she'd have to explain

what she was doing there. She was not optimistic that the police would take well to her story about seeing in one of her visions what had happened to Ellie Garfield. The first thing they'd want to know would be why, if she had information about a missing person, regardless of how she'd come by it, she hadn't come straight to the police with it. Well, she'd tell them, the police were generally very dismissive of tips from psychics, so she liked to approach the family directly. And what, the police would then ask, might you have been expecting from Mr. Garfield in exchange for this information? There was no use telling them she wanted nothing for it. They had her number. She'd come to the attention of the police during the Archer business, and a couple of her customers unhappy with their horoscope readings had been to the cops to see whether there were grounds to lay fraud charges against her. (The cops had decided that if they were to take her to court over this, they'd also have to charge every newspaper in the country.)

Given that the police were already predisposed to think poorly of her, there was every reason to believe they'd come up with another version of the events that had transpired in the Garfield home. Maybe, instead of Keisha trying to shake him down, to run a con on him, they'd think she'd just tried to rob him instead. That she'd attacked him with the knitting needle when he'd tried to stop her. The police'd believe any kind of stupid story so long as it suited their purposes.

No, calling the cops was not an option. If she could keep her name out of this, all the better.

Besides, no one could place her at the house. There were no witnesses. She hadn't told anyone she was coming here, except for Kirk, who was on standby in case she needed him for the Nina shtick. The Garfield house was on a street where the houses were well spaced out, and there was no house directly across the street. Odds were no one had seen her get out of her car and go into the house. If she could get back into her car unseen, she'd be all set.

Wendell Garfield sure wasn't going to be talking.

Then she thought: *Fingerprints*.

She wondered what she'd touched. The robe, but it wouldn't hold a fingerprint. Surely the cops couldn't lift a print off the fabric of the chair.

She wiped down the coffee table, and any other surfaces she thought she might have touched. There was plenty of blood around, but none of it was hers, so she thought she'd be okay where DNA was concerned. Once she got home, she'd change out of these blood-soaked clothes and get rid of them.

Keisha believed she could ride this out. She could do it. She'd have to wear a scarf at her neck or high collars for a few weeks to hide the bruising, but otherwise she looked unharmed.

I am done with this shit.

This whole thing, it was a message, no doubt about it. Keisha had never been a particularly religious person, but this had all the hallmarks of a warning from the man upstairs. "Knock it off," he was telling her.

She was going to knock it off.

"Lord, just let me walk out of here and I'm yours," she said.

She took one last look at the room, at Garfield's body, to be sure she hadn't missed anything. She was good. She was as sure as she could be.

Keisha slipped out of the house, wiped down the door handle on her way. She was halfway to the car when she happened to reach up and touch her right ear.

There was nothing dangling from it.

She reached up and touched her left ear. The parrot earring was there. But the other one was gone.

"Oh God," she said under her breath.

She didn't see she had much choice but to go back into that house and find it.

She walked back to the door, stood there a moment, steeling herself, then, wrapping her hand with her coat, turned the knob and entered. She started by the chair where she'd been sitting. Patted around it, stuck her fingers down into the cushion cracks.

No luck.

She looked at the coffee table, scanned the carpets. The earring was nowhere to be seen.

There was only one place left to look.

Keisha got down on her knees next to the body, slipped her hands under it, and rolled it over, revealing a carpet soaked with the blood that had poured out of Garfield's eye socket.

She spotted a small bump in the pool of blood. She stuck her fingers into it and lifted up her earring. The parrot looked like a seagull caught in a red oil spill. She wrapped the wet earring in some tissues from her purse, dropped it in, and went back out the front door.

Got in her car.

Got her keys out of her purse.

Keyed the ignition.

As she was driving away, looking ahead, she saw a police car turn the corner.

No no no no.

As it approached, Keisha wondered how visible the bloodstains splattered across the front of her clothing were. Would the cop notice them as they passed each other? For once, she was grateful for the shitty defrosters on this car. Her view through the windshield was partially obscured by crystals of frost.

The distance between the two cars closed. Keisha could see two officers in the vehicle. A woman behind the wheel, a man riding shotgun.

Just look ahead, she told herself. Like you don't care. Be cool.

The cars met.

As the police car slid past, Keisha was certain no one looked over. She kept her eyes front. Seconds later, she glanced in her rear-view mirror, expecting the patrol car's brake lights to come on, for the car to turn around, to come after her.

Lights flashing.

But nothing happened. The police car continued up the street, even going past the Garfield house.

Keisha put on her blinker, turned left at the corner. Home free.

EIGHTEEN

Rona Wedmore told dispatch she needed a couple of uniformed officers to accompany her to the Garfield house. One of their cars, she was informed, had just passed by that location. They'd return to the address and wait for Detective Wedmore's arrival.

It was possible Wendell Garfield would do as she asked, and come down to the station without protest, but you never knew, so it was good to have backup. While Garfield wasn't going to be charged with murder, he was still in a peck of trouble. He'd covered up for his daughter, he'd moved his wife's body and disposed of it, he'd misled investigators. Wedmore was even betting there was some kind of environmental pollution charge for dumping a vehicle in a lake, although that would seem to be the least of Wendell's problems.

Wedmore recognized the two police officers waiting for her. Lisa Gibson and Brett McBean. Lisa had been on the force for about a decade, Wedmore was thinking, and McBean maybe half that time. Both good cops, so far as she knew, although there was talk that since they'd been partnered six months ago, something was going on between them. Not a good thing.

Lisa got out from behind the wheel and McBean

followed suit as Wedmore pulled up. Lisa was about five foot eight, but McBean was a towering six foot five and looked like he'd have been more at home in a basketball jersey than a police uniform.

"Hey, Lisa, Brett," she said.

"Did they find his wife, Detective?" Lisa asked.

Wedmore said, "We have an idea where to look. The daughter's just confessed to killing Mrs. Garfield, and Mr. Garfield helped cover it up. I'm bringing him in. Have you noticed anything since you've been out here?"

They both shook their heads. "He hasn't come out," Brett said. "Officer Gibson just said she hasn't even noticed a curtain move since we got here."

Officer Gibson, Wedmore thought. That was all the proof she needed that these two were an item.

"Let's just play this as a straight visit," Wedmore said. "Garfield doesn't know his daughter came into the station and made a confession. So far as he knows, we're here with an update."

The two cops nodded, and followed Detective Wedmore to the door. She rang the bell while Gibson and McBean stood symbolically behind her.

There was no answer.

Wedmore rang the bell a second time, glancing over her shoulder to take note that Garfield's Buick was in the drive. When still no one answered, Officer Gibson said, "Maybe he's in the shower."

McBean said, "Check it out."

Gibson and Wedmore looked at him, saw that he was staring straight down, and followed his gaze.

There were several dark drops of something on the flagstones.

"From way up here, that looks like blood," McBean said.

As Wedmore knelt down, she reached into her pocket for a latex glove, snapped it onto her right hand, and touched the tip of her index finger to one of the drops. She gave it the briefest of inspections, looked up and said to McBean, "You go around the back of the house. Lisa, you stay with me."

McBean gave his partner a look, and went.

Wedmore stood, pulled a tissue from her pocket and wiped off the end of her index finger, but kept the glove on. She wadded the tissue, tucked it back into her pocket, then pulled back her jacket to reveal the holstered gun attached to her belt. She took it out, held it pointed down at her side, and tried the doorbell one more time.

She waited ten seconds, then reached for the knob and turned it slowly to see whether the door was locked.

It was not.

She pushed it wide and called out, "Mr. Garfield! Mr. Garfield, are you home? It's Detective Wedmore!"

Wedmore only needed to take one step into the foyer to see what was awaiting her in the living room.

"Jesus," she said.

Her eyes fixed on Wendell Garfield's body, the pool of blood around his head, some kind of long blue stick coming straight out of his eye socket.

"Oh God," said Officer Gibson, who had stepped in behind the detective.

Wedmore's hand was up in a "don't move" gesture.

"Ask McBean what's happening around back."

Gibson touched the radio clipped by her shoulder. "Anything going on out there?"

There was a crackle of static. McBean said, "Nothin'."

"Get him back here," Wedmore said.

Gibson told him they needed him around front. Seconds later, he was in the foyer, and saw what the other two were looking at.

"Fucking hell," he said.

"Secure the house," Wedmore told them.

The two of them went through the place room by room, closet by closet, and returned to the foyer a minute later to find Wedmore standing over the body, just far enough back that her shoes were not touching blood.

"House is empty," Officer Gibson said. "'Cept for him."

"What's that sticking out of his eye?" Officer McBean asked.

"Looks like a needle, for knitting," Wedmore said. It wasn't a pastime she'd ever pursued, but her late mother used to spend hours doing it. Then she saw a ball of yarn on the floor. "There ya go."

"I think I'm going to be sick," McBean said and excused himself.

Officer Gibson grimaced as her partner fled and

said to Wedmore, "He's not good with a lot of blood."

"Call this in. Get everyone out here," Wedmore said. "This scene is fresh."

Gibson went outside to make the calls.

Wedmore did a slow circle around the room, studying everything, looking for anything. She went into the kitchen and saw the pot of tea that was still warm to the touch, and the single mug that had been waiting to be filled.

"This was looking pretty simple up until about five minutes ago," Wedmore said to herself. The Ellie Garfield case had appeared to be a totally domestic affair. Daughter kills mother, father covers it up. Everyone—victim, perpetrator, accomplice after the fact—related. A family tragedy from beginning to end.

But this, well, this had the potential to change everything. Garfield's death broadened the circle. Melissa couldn't have done this, because she'd been in police custody the last couple of hours. Wedmore didn't need a forensic examiner to tell her this murder was less than two hours old. And Garfield— or at least someone claiming to be him—had phoned the station little more than an hour ago, asking for a progress report in the search for his wife.

A shrewd move, Wedmore thought. A nice way to deflect suspicion. Not that his cleverness made much difference now.

She came back to the living room, stood once again over Garfield's body. A woman's bathrobe was tossed onto the couch, but the matching sash was on the carpet, just beyond the pooling blood.

Interesting.

Then, studying the body again, looking at the blood that had saturated the man's shirt, something else caught Wedmore's eye.

"Hello?" she said under her breath. "What's this?"

NINETEEN

Kirk Nicholson was on the couch, feet up on the coffee table, having breakfast. Or an early lunch. Brunch maybe. Whatever meal it was, it consisted of a bottle of Budweiser and a cream-filled Twinkie sponge cake. He had the TV tuned in to *Family Feud*, where a family of fucking inbreds, in Kirk's estimation, was trying to guess how one hundred people had responded to the question: "What part of your body do you sometimes forget to wash when you have a bath?"

Kirk shouted: "Behind the ears!"

He was pretty good at *Family Feud*. It was his favorite game show because, unlike, say, *Jeopardy!* or *Who Wants to be a Millionaire?*, you didn't actually have to know anything, you just had to be able to guess what people *thought* the answer was. That meant Kirk often shouted out the correct response, which made him feel very good about himself.

He needed to feel better about himself these days.

Often, his gaze would move from the television to the shelf he'd set up on the adjoining wall to display the mag wheels he was going to put on his truck when the snow melted. These were 20-inch Mamba wheels, the M3 model, with eight spokes, finished in machine black. Normally, a set of four cost as much as two grand, but he'd managed to get these for three hundred off.

As much as these wheels were a sight to behold now, they were going to look awesome once they were installed. It turned out to be a blessing Keisha didn't have a garage with this pipsqueak little house of hers. If she had, he wouldn't be able to admire them every single day, and he didn't have to worry about someone breaking into a garage and stealing them. What he did have to worry about was that li'l fucker, as he now thought of Matthew, going over and touching them, getting his greasy little finger-prints on them, maybe even knocking them off the shelf and breaking the little bastard's foot.

That made him think of his own foot, which was feeling much better, thank you very much. Not that he wasn't still limping around Keisha. He wanted to keep the sympathy going for as long as possible.

Anyway, back to that little bastard. That *was* the operative word. Keisha hadn't been married when she'd had the boy, and the dad was long gone, so he felt well within his rights to call the kid a bastard, but the fact was, he liked li'l fucker better. Kirk expected the kid was going to be better behaved in the future, not touching the wheels or anything else of his, after the recent talk he'd had with him. No ten-year-old kid wanted to get sent to a military academy for pre-teens, and that was what Kirk had told the kid his mother was considering if he didn't keep his nose clean and stay out of Kirk's way.

But it was their little secret, Kirk told him. *Your ma*

doesn't know I've told you what she's thinking. Stay out of trouble, keep the noise down, stay out of the grown-ups' way, and maybe, just maybe, she'll forget the whole thing.

It was working, too. The kid had been on his best behavior lately.

"Between the toes!" he shouted at the set, coming up with another answer.

He took a swig from the beer bottle and another bite of the Twinkie. Turned out he could have stayed in bed. Never got the "Nina" call from Keisha, which he guessed meant her latest target had bought her story hook, line and sinker. He wondered how much money she'd come home with today. They needed more food in the house. He'd looked all through the fridge and hadn't found a single thing he wanted to eat. He was definitely going to have to have a talk with her.

He yawned, stared at the set like a lumbering bear. The *Feud* wasn't holding his interest. Sometimes he found it a bit hard to follow.

He was reaching for the remote when Keisha burst through the front door.

Covered in blood.

He tossed the remote onto the coffee table and swung his feet down to the floor. "What the hell?"

There was blood on her face, on her throat, all over her blouse. There was blood on her hands and arms and some on her pants, as well.

"Help me!" she screamed at him, dropping her purse to the floor, standing there like someone who'd been thrown into a pool with all their clothes on, arms sticking out to the sides, away from her body, car keys dangling from the fingers of her right hand.

He ran over, but held up when he was about a foot away, afraid to touch her, she was such a fright. Kirk hated getting his clothes all messed up. "What happened? Were you in an accident? Where you bleeding from?"

"I'm not hurt—well, I am, but the blood, the blood's not mine."

"Jesus, woman, who the hell's blood—"

"Shut up! Shut up and listen to me!"

"I'm just asking, what the fuck—"

"Shut up!" she screamed, much louder this time.

He wasn't used to letting her talk to him this way, but the circumstances seemed to dictate that he do what she said, at least for now. So he shut up.

"Get a garbage bag," she told him. "I'm takin' my clothes off right here and bagging them. Then get some newspapers and put them on the floor so I can get to the bathroom without leaving any blood anywhere."

He stood there, stunned, not moving.

"A bag!" she said. "Get a goddamn bag!"

Kirk ran into the kitchen and returned with a green garbage bag with a red plastic tie threaded into the top. Keisha dropped her keys to the floor and started to unbutton her blouse. She opened it up, slid the blood-soaked sleeves down her arms and dropped the top into the bag as Kirk held it open. Blood had soaked through her blouse and stained her white bra. She reached around her back, unsnapped it, slipped the straps off her shoulders and dropped the under-garment into the bag, noticing that even now, in the midst of something horrible Kirk still had no under-standing of, he still took a second to look at her tits.

She slipped off her shoes, unzipped her pants, stepped out of them, panties too. Dropped everything into the bag.

She stood there, stark naked, and said, "Hand me the bag. Get the newspaper."

Kirk wasn't a newspaper reader, but Keisha always maintained a subscription to the *Register* for leads on possible clients. There was a stack of them under the coffee table and Kirk used half a dozen to make a path over the carpeting to the bathroom.

"Baby, you gotta tell me what happened," he said as she walked tentatively down the hall.

"I went to see that guy, whose wife disappeared last week," she said. "The one I had you on standby for?"

Kirk nodded. "Yeah. The one on the TV with his daughter."

"That's right. The son of a bitch *did it*. He killed his wife. He thought I'd figured it out and he tried to kill me." She was in the bathroom now, looking at herself in the mirror. "You see the marks on my neck here?" She ran her hands under the tap, tried to wipe away the blood on her throat.

"Holy shit. He tried to strangle you?"

"Yeah. He'd just about finished me off when I got hold of this knitting needle and swung it back and got him in the eye."

Kirk winced. "In the fucking *eye*?"

"That made him let go of me," Keisha said, reaching into the shower to turn on the hot and cold taps.

"Wait, what are you saying?" Kirk asked. "You left the guy with this needle sticking out of his head? Did he go to the hospital?"

"He's dead, Kirk."

His head snapped back. "What?"

"He's dead. This is what you have to do. You have to get rid of my clothes. At first I was thinking, burn them out back, but the cops, I've seen those shows, they can find blood on burned-up clothes, I'm sure of it. So you got to take that bag and drive somewhere far away, like go to Darien or Stamford or somewhere and throw that bag into a Dumpster with a thousand other bags, just someplace where no one is ever going to find it, you got that?"

"You *killed* this guy?"

"Are you listening?"

She stuck her hand in the water to test the temperature. She turned up the hot tap. She was going to burn this blood off her.

"Yeah, okay, I'm listening."

"Once you get rid of the bag, you're going to have to wipe down the car. Like the door handles, the seat. They're vinyl, so anything on them you should be able to get off."

Kirk was stupefied, shaking his head, still clutching the bag in his hand.

"Kirk, are you there?"

"Yeah, yeah, I'm here."

"You understand what you have to do?"

"Get rid of your clothes, wash the car."

"Not just *wash* it. You've got to go all over it. Like you were getting ready to sell it. Like you were cleaning your *truck*."

"Yeah, okay."

"Shit, and my purse, too. Go get my purse."

Keisha could hear his footsteps on the newsprint. She called out to him: "If you walk on the paper, you're going to get blood on your shoes!"

"Oh, yeah." A pause. "They look okay!"

He returned with her purse, smeared with Wendell Garfield's blood. She took it from him and said, "Put all the newspapers into the bag." He gave her a look that suggested he was tired of taking orders, but went.

She dumped the contents of the purse onto the floor. It had been on the floor by the chair she'd been sitting in at the Garfield house. When she'd thrust that needle over her shoulder and caught Wendell Garfield's eye, blood had sprayed everywhere, some of it landing in the open purse. Tissues, her wallet, lipstick, chewing gum, a small container of Tylenol—almost everything had some small trace of it.

And there was that bloody parrot earring.

She grabbed her wallet, which contained her driver's license, cards for everything from Social Security to Visa—even a Subway sandwich card—and set it on the counter by the sink. She saw Garfield's cash tucked into the small pouch, ran her bloody hand under the tap and fished it out. A few droplets of blood. She'd go through the bills later, see if any of them could be saved. She'd have to throw out the check, of course, with Garfield's name and signature on it, but not now. She couldn't trust that Kirk, if he got his hands on it, wouldn't be dumb enough to try and cash it.

Quickly, before he returned, she tucked the money in the cabinet under the sink, behind some extra rolls of toilet paper.

Kirk returned.

"All this stuff," she said, pointing to the items on the floor, including the tissues, lipstick and gum, "has to be thrown out."

Kirk scooped the items off the tile floor, shoved them into the bag. "I think that's everything."

"I dropped my keys by the door. You're going to have to rinse those off."

"Yeah." His eyes held hers. "So, just what kind of shit you getting me into here, babe? Am I, like, covering up a murder?"

"He was going to kill me if I didn't kill him."

"Well, I guess then, it's cool." He certainly wasn't inclined to call the police. If they came and arrested Keisha, what would happen to him? Would he have to look after her kid? Would he have to go live someplace if she lost her house? If she got taken away and wasn't making any money, how was he going to live? How would he pay for improvements to his truck?

No, turning her in was not an option.

"Kirk, you can do this, right?" she asked. "You can get rid of that bag?"

He gave her a smile, but his eyes looked dull. "Hey, I scratch your back, you scratch mine, right?"

Keisha didn't like the sound of that, but right now, Kirk was all she had. She needed him to do these things for her, and she needed him to do them right now.

He left the bathroom. She listened until she heard him pull the front door closed. As she was about to step under the spray, it hit her, everything that had happened in the last hour, and she took two hurried steps to the toilet, lifted the lid frantically, dropped to her knees and threw up. Three good heaves.

She unrolled a couple of feet of toilet paper, dabbed her face, flushed the toilet, and allowed her body to collapse against the cold tiled wall.

I nearly died.

I killed a man.

Her breathing was quick and shallow, and she wondered whether she might pass out. Hold it together, she thought. Suck it up. Kirk would get rid of the evidence, clean the car.

She hoped to God he didn't fuck it up. It wasn't like she'd sent him to the store with a list of ingredients to make rocket fuel. He ought to be able to wash a car and get rid of a bag.

Slowly she pulled herself to her feet and got into the shower. The hot water felt good hitting her skin. She poured some shampoo into her hand, washed her hair, rinsed, shampooed it again. Then a third time.

By the time she picked up the soap to start on her body, the blood was washed away, but that didn't stop her from nearly scrubbing herself raw.

She stood under the water until it started to go cold. When there was no hot left, she turned off the taps, reached beyond the curtain for the towel, and dried herself off.

Out of the shower, she studied her naked body in the mirror. She thought there was a tiny spot of blood on her right shoulder, rubbed it with the towel, realized it was a mole.

She was confident she'd gotten every trace of Wendell Garfield off her.

Still naked, she gathered up the towel and bathmat and walked it down to the basement, shoved everything into the washing machine, poured in some soap, and hit the start button.

Back upstairs, she went into her room and dressed herself in fresh clothes. She found a blouse with a high collar, which she buttoned to the top to hide the bruises on her neck. Then she slowly walked the route between the front door and the bathroom, looking for any traces of blood. The newspaper seemed to have done the trick. She got some paper towel and Windex from underneath the kitchen sink and squirted the tiles inside the front door. She cleaned them three times, just to be sure, then flushed the paper towels, one at a time so as not to cause a clog, down the toilet.

Then she thought, what about when she ran from the car to the house? It was such a short distance, she was confident no one had seen her. If anyone had, they'd surely have called the police. But there might be blood out there.

She opened the door. The light snow that had fallen overnight had melted on the driveway and the path from it to the house, but everything was so wet, she didn't think, even if some blood had somehow dripped from her clothes, that anyone would be able to find a trace of it out here.

She went back inside, picked up her wallet by the sink, and rubbed it all over with several dampened tissues. Took out her driver's license, Social Security card. Made sure everything was clean.

Then she leaned against the bathroom counter, put her face in her hands, felt some relief slowly washing over her. She was done. So long as Kirk did as he was told, she was good.

Time for a drink.

As she entered the kitchen, the phone rang. It wasn't a sound that normally made Keisha jump, but she nearly hit the ceiling on that first ring. She looked at the caller ID, but it came up as unknown.

No one knows. No one knows anything about what happened. Certainly not yet.

Keisha picked up. "Hello?"

"Oh, hey, Keisha? It's Chad and—"

The health store owner in Bridgeport who needed her advice every time he met a new man. "Chad, I don't have time today."

"But I met this guy, he came into the store, and I think we kind of clicked, and I found out his birth

165

date and I'm not sure we're compatible because I'm a Virgo and—"

"Not today," Keisha said and hung up.

She opened the fridge. She needed something strong to drink but there was nothing in there but Kirk's bottles of Bud. That would have to do. She plunked herself down in a chair, cracked open a bottle, and took a long swig.

Never again, she told herself. *Never again*.

The thing was, Keisha didn't know what other line of work she was suited for. Sales? Working in a department store? Greeting people as they came into Walmart? Didn't you have to be a hundred to do that? Yeah, she'd cleaned houses once in a while, but even that was never entirely honest work for Keisha Ceylon. She found it hard not to take a peek into the backs of dresser drawers, in case there was something valuable stashed there, something she could help herself to that when the owner finally went to look for it, they'd have no idea when it actually went missing.

She wanted to blame her dead mother at times like this, but Keisha knew, in her heart, that she was an adult now and responsible for her choices. The good ones, like keeping Matthew and doing her best by him even when his father didn't give a damn. And the bad ones, like getting taken in by Kirk's charm, and now having to live with the consequences. But Jesus, her mother really was a piece of work, and Keisha felt entitled to lay at least some of the blame at her door.

The way they lived. Always moving from town to town, Marjorie surveying the local papers for obituaries to find men who'd recently lost their wives and just happening to show up on their doorstep, offering her services as a housekeeper, but not before putting on her lipstick, letting her hair fall down around her shoulders, and unbuttoning that top button on her blouse. "Your wife just died?" she'd say, with a hint of Alabama in her voice. "I had no idea I was troubling you at such a time. I'm just looking for some work to support myself and my daughter here, but I won't trouble you a moment longer . . . What's that? Why, I must confess, I wouldn't mind a glass of lemonade."

Marjorie'd worm her way into some lonely man's heart just long enough to gain his trust, and access to his bank account.

And then they were off to the next town.

"Can't we live in one place for a while?" Keisha'd ask her mom. "So I could go to school and make friends?"

The longest they stayed anywhere was when Marjorie got a job managing a rooming house in Middlebury where almost all the residents were elderly, living alone, and scraping by on their Social Security checks, out of which they paid the rent. Marjorie had been thinking of quitting—the owner, who lived down in Florida, didn't pay her much to run the joint—but then one of the residents died in his sleep one night, and Marjorie had an epiphany. If she didn't report poor old Garnett's death, and got rid of his body, she could cash, and keep, his Social Security checks when they arrived each month. If she rented out the room to someone else, she could pocket the entire amount.

With Keisha's help—the girl was now in her teens—Marjorie removed the body from the house late one night and buried it in the woods outside Middlebury. It was Keisha's job to endorse the checks when they came—her mother, who had a very shaky hand, was very particular that the signature look just like Garnett's, and made Keisha practise over and over again before actually signing the check.

Over the next six months, two more residents died. The scam expanded. Marjorie now had three Social Security checks coming in, plus her wage for managing the rooming house.

A pretty good living, until one day a woman dropped by, looking to reconnect with her long-lost uncle Garnett, and when she couldn't find him, said she was heading to the police station to file a missing person report.

"Pack your bags," Marjorie had whispered to her daughter the moment the woman left. "We're leaving town in five minutes."

The police never did catch up with her. When Marjorie died, of liver cancer, she'd never spent a single day in jail.

Keisha'd known it was wrong, but what was she supposed to do? Turn her mother in? Then what?

So maybe the cards were stacked against her when it came to making an honest buck, but today, well, today was one hell of a wake-up call. Surely there had to be something she could do—something legitimate—that employed her skills.

Politics, maybe.

She almost laughed. The thing was, what she'd been doing with all her variations on a theme was selling people outrageous notions. That she could help them talk to deceased relatives. That she could give them a glimpse of their future by reading the stars. That she could use her psychic gifts to help track down missing loved ones.

If she could sell people that kind of malarkey, how hard could cars be? Or insurance? Or carpeting?

Keisha told herself she could do it. She had to do it. Not for herself, but for Matthew.

She couldn't be much of a mother from behind bars.

She had to turn over that proverbial new leaf. She had to rid herself of Kirk. But first, she had to get out of this current mess she'd gotten herself into. Then, she could start thinking about a new career. Get herself some new clothes. Less funky, more conservative. No parrot earrings. Maybe a different hairdo. A more professional look. And of course, she'd have to get some new business—

No. No no no no no.

She'd given him her business card. Wendell Garfield had tucked it into his shirt pocket.

TWENTY

Kirk opened the passenger door of Keisha's fifteen-year-old Korean shitbox and set the trash bag on the floor ahead of the seat. The vinyl upholstery was tan, so there was no trick to spotting the blood smears on the driver's seat. He fetched a container of already dampened cloths in his truck—he had a full supply of automotive cleaning supplies tucked behind the seats—and used the first one to wipe down the handle on the driver's door of Keisha's car. Once he'd cleaned the grab handle on the inside of the door, he turned his attention to the seat. He went through a couple of dozen cloths, jamming them into the cracks and crevices of the cushioning. There wasn't all that much blood, but he knew there wouldn't have to be for the cops to nail Keisha. He didn't just watch *Family Feud*. He knew stuff.

He found heavier concentrations of blood when he wiped down the steering wheel. Keisha'd had it all over her hands, of course. He took all the bloodied cloths and stuffed them into the bag, which had not yet been tied off. Once he was confident the car's interior was not only wiped clean of blood, but cleaner than it had been since it left the showroom, he knotted the top of the bag with the built-in red ties and settled into the driver's seat, still glistening from the wipes.

It struck him it might be a good idea to get the entire car washed while he was at it. There was one of those do-it-yourself places up on Route 1. He searched his pockets to confirm that he had enough coins. He'd get Keisha to pay him back later.

He drove the car into a wash bay. He had his choice of all of them. Hardly anyone was washing their cars when there'd been snow overnight and the streets were wet and slushy. He plunked in some quarters and trained the high-pressure hose on the driver's side of the car. Back and forth along the door, just to be sure.

When he was finished, he got on the turnpike and headed west. At first, he was thinking he'd go as far as Westport, or maybe even Norwalk, but he hadn't even gotten to Bridgeport when he started thinking this was a really dumb idea of Keisha's. A bag of garbage was a bag of garbage, even when it was stuffed with a lot of bloody clothes. As long as he dumped it in with plenty of other bags, he didn't see the sense in driving it halfway across the goddamn state. Any Dumpster ought to do.

So he got off at Seaview and went north, keeping his eye out for a strip mall that would have a garbage bin out back. He'd be able to ditch the trash, get back to Keisha's house within the hour, and find out a little more about this mess she'd gotten herself into. God, she could be dumb sometimes.

Living with her, you just never knew what was

going to happen. All sorts of weird folks dropping by, wanting Keisha to tell them whether to quit their jobs or get married or try to reach their dead cats so they could say hello, taking as gospel some mumbo-jumbo bullshit that Keisha just came up with out of her head. And, once in a while, when some kid got abducted or an Alzheimer's patient wandered out of the nursing home, anxious relatives—at least those who believed in any of that other aforementioned nonsense—would ask for Keisha's guidance.

People sure believed some strange shit.

Kirk did his part, playing the father whose missing daughter Keisha'd found based on a vision. He thought he did a good job at it, so long as the people didn't ask too many questions. Once he started lying, he found it hard to remember everything he'd already said, laying traps for himself. So he'd keep it short, pretend to get all choked up and say, "That woman, Keisha, she's the reason our little angel was brought home to us. I can't even think what might have happened if she hadn't been there for us."

Oscar-worthy.

Life was never boring with Keisha, but son of a bitch, she'd really raised the bar this time. From what she'd had time to tell him as she did her striptease, she'd killed this guy in self-defense with a knitting needle in the eye.

Fucking *eye*, man. He could not get over that.

He couldn't have predicted, when he'd moved in with Keisha, anything like this. He could see that it wasn't going to be perfect, what with her having the kid and all, but he didn't seem all that annoying at first, and Keisha was pretty awesome in the sack. She said she was taking precautions so he wouldn't knock her up, not like when she'd had that thing eleven years ago with a soldier home on leave from Afghanistan who hung around Milford long enough to spread his seed. Then he was back on the plane to blow up some more Taliban. Keisha didn't know whether he kept signing up for more tours because he really liked riding around in a tank in a hundred and twenty degrees, or because he didn't want to face the fact that back home he was a father.

Matthew'd only met the man twice in nine years. Which was one more time than he'd sent home money. That one time, it had been for $123.43.

Keisha, however, was doubly devoted to the li'l fucker. Okay, maybe he wasn't that bad a kid really, but the fact was, he was *there*. Kind of hard to have one's needs met when there's some twerp hanging around, playing Wii, asking to be taken to the mall, coming down with colds and expecting his mother to look after him. And lots of times she'd make his breakfast or a sandwich or take him a snack at bedtime, and she wouldn't even *think* to ask Kirk if he'd like something too.

Still, it had been a good plan, moving in with Keisha. He'd been as nice as he could be when he met her, helping her with that flat tire. And it was no act, his treating her with respect. She had it going on. Nice bod, pretty face. That first night at her place, he found out she could cook a half-decent meal, too. He

174

went slow, not wanting her to think the only thing he cared about was getting into her pants, but once she told him the kid was asleep, he knew she wanted it, and he was happy to oblige. The thing Kirk never got around to mentioning was, he didn't actually have a place of his own. He'd gotten the boot from his ex-girlfriend, and had taken to sleeping on the couches of various guys who worked for Garber Contracting, except for Glen himself, who wasn't taking in boarders when he had a young girl in the house, no offense intended. He couldn't keep doing that forever, so when Keisha started hinting that since he was staying over most nights anyway, maybe he should just . . .

"Yeah, okay," he'd said.

Things were okay those first few weeks, before Glen cut back his hours. Then he hurt his foot, and in some ways that came at a good time, because he could tell Keisha had been starting to reassess, to wonder if maybe inviting him into her home had been such a great idea after all. She wasn't going to kick him out while he was recovering. She was too nice to do that.

And now, his foot pretty much healed, he was sensing she might be thinking, once again, about dissolving this relationship. But now, well, she *needed* him now. Big time. What woman is going to throw out onto the street the man who's helping her cover up a murder?

Oh yeah, he was in for the long haul. No doubt about that.

Hey, that looked like a good spot.

A short plaza on the right with a nail salon, a takeout-only pizza place, a T-shirt operation, and a shop that sold radio-controlled cars.

Always wanted to get one of those, Kirk thought. *Now that I've got my wheels for the truck, time to treat myself to something else.*

A row of shops like this had to have some kind of Dumpster out back, especially with the pizza joint. They'd have a lot of trash, right? Leftover food at the end of the day, cardboard, cheese that had gone moldy?

He hit the blinker, turned into the lot, drove down the side of the building and around back, coming to a stop by a battered metal refuse container the size of this shitbox car he was driving. It sat about thirty feet out from the building, and was surrounded by other trash. Abandoned pallets, scraps of rusted pipe, an old oven, half a dozen tires.

Kirk got out and came around to the passenger side of the car. He opened the door, grabbed the bag, and approached the container. He was about to lift the lid and toss it in when he was interrupted.

"The hell you doing?"

One of the four back doors was open. Judging from its position, Kirk guessed it was the rear entry to the pizza place. A black man in jeans, a black T-shirt and white apron splotched with pizza sauce was looking at him.

"Just throwing this in," Kirk said.

"No. You're not."

"It's just one bag. Chill out, man."

"What, you think our bin's here for your convenience? You got garbage, put it out front of your own yard."

"Hey, pal, why don't—"

"Don't fucking 'pal' me, asshole. We pay to get this trash hauled away. You want to put that bag in? Ten bucks." He stepped forward, allowing the metal door to swing shut behind him. "People like you doing this all the time. Thinking this is a public dump. You got ten bucks?"

"Yeah, I do. And you know where you can put it?" Kirk asked.

The pizza guy laughed. "Oh, that's good. And I got an idea where you can put that bag of trash."

He'd closed the distance between them. Kirk still had one hand on the bag, the other on the metal lid, but he hadn't raised it far enough to toss the bag in. The other man slapped his hand on top of it and it slammed shut with a resounding clang. If Kirk hadn't yanked his hand away quickly enough, he'd be minus a thumb.

"What's your problem?" Kirk asked. He thought of a good *Family Feud* question: "Name a place where dickheads are most likely to work?" He'd shout: "Takeout pizza joint!"

But what he said was, "You got a pepperoni stick up your ass or something?" He really wanted to have a go at this guy. Kick his ass good.

"This what you want?" the man asked. "You want to get into it over this? Because if that's what you want, then that's okay by me."

The bag concealing the bloody clothes and bloody purse and bloody cleaning clothes dropped from Kirk's hand to the asphalt so he'd have both fists ready.

The back door to the pizza place opened again, and a second man came out. White guy, about twice the size of the black guy.

Kirk thought, *Shit.*

"Hey, Mick, help me out with this asshole!" the black guy said.

If it mattered to Mick that he had no idea what this dispute was about, he showed no sign. He was too busy looking, immediately, for something to use to hit Kirk, and he found it up against the wall. A discarded two-foot length of lead pipe. He raised it like a club, looked at Kirk, and smiled.

Kirk bolted.

He jumped back into the car, slammed the door, did a fast three-point turn, narrowly missing Mick as the front end swung past him in reverse, then floored it, racing back up the side of the building and onto the street.

He was two blocks away before he realized he'd left the bag sitting there next to the Dumpster.

TWENTY-ONE

The crime scene people had arrived at the Garfield house. Rona Wedmore stepped back so they could do their job. Eight uniformed officers had also shown up, and Wedmore had them fanned out across the neighborhood, knocking on doors, trying to find anyone who might have seen anything. The last thing she did before leaving was ask Joy Bennings, the lead crime scene investigator, to let her know what was on the card she'd noticed tucked into Wendell Garfield's shirt. Wedmore had been able to make out a couple of digits—the beginning of a phone number—in one corner, but that was it. She'd left it in the shirt. Smeared with blood that might not be the victim's own, she didn't want to interfere with it. She asked Joy to call her the moment she was able to make out what the card said.

Then she got in her car and drove back to the station so that she could have a further conversation with Melissa.

But on her way to see Melissa, she was told a Mrs. Beaudry was waiting to see her. She'd identified herself at the front desk as Melissa's aunt, said that she had come to the station looking for Melissa or her father.

Wedmore found the woman pacing in the station

lobby. Mid-forties, not much more than five feet, with a tiny frame and a long, hooked nose. She looked, Wedmore thought, bird-like. If you squeezed her too tight, she'd break in your arms.

"Excuse me," Wedmore said. "You're Mrs. Beaudry? Are you Melissa Garfield's aunt?"

The woman's eyes went wide with expectation. "Yes! I've been waiting to talk to someone about—"

"You're Ellie Garfield's sister?"

"No, I'm Wendell's sister. I'm Gail. I tried to reach Wendell at the house and when there was no answer—he doesn't own a cell phone—I figured they were both down here. And all they'll tell me is that Melissa is here but not her father and they won't let me talk to her. What's going on?"

"Would you like to sit down, Mrs. Beaudry?"

"No, I would not like to sit down! Where's Melissa? Is she okay? Her father's not with her?"

"Melissa's perfectly safe. I need to ask you some questions, Mrs. Beaudry."

"About what?"

"About Melissa, and your brother, and Ellie."

The woman, baffled, awaited the first question.

"When did you last talk to your brother?" Wedmore asked.

She looked at the detective, puzzled. "Why?"

"Mrs. Beaudry, please. When's the last time you spoke?"

"Last night. I called him before I went to bed to see whether he'd heard anything."

"You didn't speak to him at all today?"

"No."

"What about Melissa? Have you had any conversations with her in the last twenty-four hours?"

"I saw both of them at the press conference. For moral support. But I haven't talked to her since then."

"What can you tell me about her state of mind?" Wedmore asked.

"She's distraught, of course! Who wouldn't be?"

"Did she say anything to you?"

"No, not really. I just told her, and Wendell, we'd do anything we could to help. Like them, we just want Ellie to come home safe and sound."

Wedmore nodded. "I see. And about Wendell . . ."

"Yes?"

"Do you know whether your brother was involved in any business deals, any personal relationships, where he might have made enemies?"

"No, no, of course not."

"You're unaware of anyone who might be angry with your brother for any reason?" Even as she asked the question, Wedmore thought about Laci Harmon's husband. She'd said he didn't know about the affair. But what if he did? What if he went to Garfield's house to confront him?

But wait. Laci Harmon had told Wedmore that morning that her husband was driving back from Schenectady. With the kids. Wedmore would want to double-check that, but it made her think the husband probably wasn't a suspect.

"What on earth are you getting at? Why are you

asking these questions? Shouldn't you people be looking for Ellie? Shouldn't you be finding out what's
happened to her?"

Wedmore took a long breath. "Mrs. Beaudry,
I'm sorry to have to tell you this, but your brother's
dead."

Gail Beaudry cocked her head, like a dog who'd
heard a whistle. "Wendell's—what?"

"Your brother is dead. He died this morning. In
the last few hours." She reached out and touched the
woman's arm. "I'm very sorry."

The woman needed a moment for this to sink
in. "How do you know? Is he here? Where did it
happen? At home? Did he have a heart attack? Oh
God, he probably had a heart attack. Is that what
happened? Was it a stroke? That's probably what
happened. The stress of all this, of not knowing what's
happened to Ellie, oh no oh no . . ."

"It wasn't a heart attack," Wedmore said gently.
"And it wasn't a stroke. Your brother is a homicide
victim."

"He's—he's a what?"

"Someone killed him, Mrs. Beaudry."

The woman put her hand to her chest and gasped.
"Dear God. First Ellie disappears, and now Wendell
is *dead*?" A flash seemed to go off in her head. "Does
this mean—oh no—does this mean Ellie's been murdered too?"

Wedmore hesitated. "In fact, we believe so, yes."

Gail struggled to comprehend the news. That two
members of her family were dead. She took several

seconds to catch her breath. "So there's someone roaming around out there, someone who's killed Ellie and Wendell?"

Wedmore steeled herself. She was going to have to get to it sooner or later. "Whoever killed your brother, yes, that person is still out there."

"I don't . . . I don't understand."

"The facts we have so far suggest your brother and sister-in-law were killed by different people. In totally separate circumstances."

"Different people?" Gail Beaudry was starting to put something together. "You said whoever killed Wendell is still out there, but you didn't say that about Ellie. You have the man who killed Ellie?"

It struck Wedmore as natural that Gail Beaudry would assume a man had killed her sister-in-law. Most killers were men.

"Mrs. Beaudry," Wedmore said, "we're going to be charging Melissa with your sister-in-law's death. The reason you can't see her is because she's in custody."

The woman took no time at all to react to this. "That's ridiculous. That's not true. That's absolutely preposterous."

"I'm afraid not," Rona Wedmore said.

"She'd never do such a thing. Never! Melissa and her mother were very close. I've never heard anything so outrageous. For heaven's sake, whatever evidence you think you have, I'm sure there's an explanation. Talk to the girl! She'll set you straight."

"Melissa has confessed," Detective Wedmore said. "She came in here of her own accord." Gail was speechless, so Wedmore added, "But she was here, in this building, when her father was killed. We don't know what the connection is."

"This is crazy, insane. I have to . . . I have to call someone." Gail Beaudry fumbled in her purse for her phone. "And my husband, I'm going to have to call my husband."

Wedmore excused herself. She had to go back and see Melissa again.

The girl howled like a wounded animal.

She threw her arms around Detective Wedmore, put her face on her chest and sobbed. "No, no, no."

It wasn't, strictly speaking, procedure to take murder suspects into one's arms and comfort them, but Wedmore found herself doing just that. She placed her hands on the girl's back and patted her ever so gently, thinking to herself what a pathetic gesture it was. Might as well be saying, "There, there."

"Daddy," she whimpered. "Daddy."

"I have to ask you some questions, Melissa," Wedmore said.

But the girl continued to weep, and it was ten minutes before Wedmore could get her back into the chair in the interrogation room. Instead of facing her from across the table, she brought her own chair around next to Melissa's and allowed the girl to hold onto her hands.

"Someone killed him?" Melissa asked disbelievingly. "Are you sure?"

Wedmore thought back to what she'd seen.

"Yes," she said with certainty. "What haven't you told me, Melissa? What aren't you telling me?"

"I've told you everything, I swear."

"Who would want to hurt your father?"

"No one. *Nobody*."

"Did someone else help you, Melissa? Was there a third person involved in getting your mother, and the car, up to the lake?"

"No, I'm telling you, it was just me and Dad. And he didn't even hurt Mom. That was me, that was all me."

"What about the man who's the father of your child?"

"Lester?"

"That's right. Did he and your father get along? Is it possible they could have had some kind of argument?"

"My parents *liked* Lester," Melissa said. "They were mad at me because I didn't want to marry him." She put her face in her hands again and wept.

Wedmore sighed, and got up.

This was the damnedest thing she'd dealt with in a while.

She was just leaving the interrogation room when her phone buzzed. It was a text, from Joy.

It read: "Got something. Call me."

TWENTY-TWO

Keisha tried to think how she would explain it.

Because she *would* have to explain it. There was no doubt in her mind. The police would eventually find Wendell Garfield, if they hadn't already, and sooner or later they'd discover her business card, tucked into his shirt pocket.

If the card had been anywhere else—in a drawer, in his wallet, even—it wouldn't have been such a big deal. Over time, everyone collects lots of business cards. You find them in your car, your coat pocket, pinned to bulletin boards.

But a card that's been tucked into a shirt, well, that's a card that has to have been acquired, or at the very least referred to, very recently. Assuming that Wendell Garfield did not wear the same, unlaundered shirt for days or weeks on end, it would be reasonable for the police to assume he'd acquired, or been looking at, that card in the last couple of days. Since his wife had gone missing.

And how did most people acquire cards? From the people whose name was on them.

It was just a matter of time before the police would be at Keisha's door, asking whether she'd met with Wendell Garfield. When was this meeting? Where was it held? What was its purpose and who had initiated it?

What would she tell them?

"I have no idea how he got that card."

That's what she would tell them.

It might be a hard story to stick to, but now that Kirk had gotten rid of everything else linking her to the Garfield house, she believed she could ride it out.

She'd tell them that she often left her cards pinned to noticeboards in grocery stores. Sometimes she'd leave a few out on tables at craft shows and community center events. She'd distribute them to random people she might meet waiting in a checkout line, or at a bus stop.

The cards were out there, she'd say. Who knows where he might have gotten one?

Maybe he'd come across one weeks ago, put it in a drawer, and after his wife disappeared, he went hunting for it, thinking maybe a psychic could assist him in ways the police had not. He'd found the card and slipped it into his shirt, and probably would have called her if he hadn't ended up with a knitting needle in his brain.

Of course, only Keisha knew it would have made no sense for Garfield to engage the services of a psychic to find his wife. He knew all about his wife's fate. But the police didn't know that, did they? So far as they were aware, Wendell Garfield was still a distraught husband desperate for his wife's return. Maybe the police would even start working on the theory that whoever got rid of Ellie—at some point they'd conclude that she was the victim of foul play, even if they never found her body at the bottom of that lake—was the same person who'd killed her husband.

That would make sense, right?

And really, what did her business card have to do with all that?

It's just a card.

She tried to tell herself not to worry about it. Play dumb, stonewall, act perplexed. However he came into possession of her card, it wasn't her responsibility to explain it.

The phone rang.

Keisha looked at it but did not move. Probably Chad calling back, or some other needy client. Let it go to message, which it would do after five rings. The ringing stopped, and Keisha waited for the light to flash to indicate a message had indeed been left, but the light never flashed.

Just as well, she thought.

There was a loud rattling at the front door, then the sound of it opening. Keisha jumped almost as much as she had the first time the phone had rung.

Who the hell was this? Wasn't it too soon for Kirk to be back?

"Hey, babe!" he called out.

Keisha met him in the hall. "What are you doing here?"

"Whaddya mean?"

"Where did you go? Where'd you get rid of it?"

"It's all taken care of," he said, waving his hand dismissively.

"Okay, but where?"

"I did what you asked, okay? It's done." He tried to get past her to go into the kitchen, but she laid her palm on his chest.

"I told you to take it to Darien or someplace far. You didn't go that far, did you? You're back too soon."

"Well shit, that was just a stupid idea you had. I mean, the main thing is, don't dump it in your backyard, right? Just because you don't want to put it out in front of your house on pickup day doesn't mean you got to drive it to hell and back."

Keisha shook her head angrily. "Where did you toss it?"

He waved her off. "Look, you owe me some money. I had some expenses, at the car wash. Used every quarter I had."

"Where did you ditch the bag?" It came out more like a scream than a question.

"Jesus, don't get your panties in a knot. Almost all the way to Bridgeport," he said.

"What did I tell you?"

"I heard what you said, but once I was out there, I had decisions to make. I saw a good spot behind this strip of stores so that was where I left it."

She shook her head in exasperation. "I swear to God. Did you at least shove it way down into the Dumpster with a bunch of other bags?"

Kirk hesitated.

"What?" Keisha asked.

He shrugged. "Pretty much."

"What do you mean, pretty much?"

"Okay, so I drive behind this place and I'm getting ready to put the bag in the Dumpster, right? Then this asshole comes out the back door of this pizza place and starts giving me attitude about putting my trash in his bin, so—"

"Wait a minute? He *saw* you? And the *car*? He saw you putting the bag in there?"

"God, woman, let me finish," Kirk said. Keisha was really starting to get on his nerves. "So anyway, the guy's all in my face about it, and I'm thinking, what's the big deal, one lousy bag of garbage, so what if I dump it in his bin, you know? So he's acting like he wants to get into it, which is okay by me, but then some other guy the size of a refrigerator comes out to back him up and he's swinging this fucking pipe like a baseball bat, so I had to get the hell out of there. I can take on one guy, no problem, but two, that's a bit much."

"Oh my God," Keisha said. "Do you think they called the police?"

He shrugged. "Why would they do that? A fight over a bag of garbage? Who's going to call the cops for that? It's a couple of pizza guys. Don't worry about it."

Keisha was *very* worried. What if they made a note of the license number of her car?

She asked, "So where did you end up putting the bag?"

"Okay, so here's the thing," Kirk said. "When that shithead started coming at me with the pipe, I had to take off, right then. So I left the bag there."

"You left it there? Where they'd seen you?"

"That guy would have killed me with that pipe," Kirk said.

Keisha was wishing he had. "Tell me you at least got the bag way in there before all this happened. I mean, nobody's going to want to go into a Dumpster after a specific bag. Not after you're gone."

Kirk made a funny face and ran his hand over his chin. "Well, I'd agree with you on that if that was the way it happened. But I never actually got the bag into the Dumpster."

"What?"

"I had to leave it on the ground. When that guy started coming after me. Asshole would have busted my head open."

Was the floor tilting? Were they in the middle of an earthquake? Things seemed to be swaying to Keisha. "You're telling me you left it there? Right there? *In front of them*? Shit, why didn't you just empty the bag out so they could get a real good look? What the hell were you—"

I've had just about enough of this, he thought.

He exploded, throwing her up against the wall so hard it knocked the wind out of her. He wrapped his right hand around her throat, pinning her head to the wall, squeezing her right where the pink sash had bit into her skin.

"I am sick and tired of you criticizing me," he said

through gritted teeth. "I am trying to help you out here and getting no thanks in return and it's starting to get on my nerves."

"Let . . . go . . . Can't . . ."

Keisha raised her leg, tried to knee Kirk in the groin. He jumped back, let go of her neck. Keisha doubled over, coughed several times.

"I'm not taking any more shit from you," he told her, jabbing his finger in her direction. "I've been helping you out here, helping you raise that kid, looking out for you, and you don't give me an ounce of respect."

Even as she coughed, Keisha managed to laugh. "Yeah, you're invaluable," she said. "You're just fucking indispensable."

He pointed that menacing finger right at her face, only inches from the end of her nose. "That's just what I'm talking about! Attitude! How's that l'il fucker of yours going to show me any respect when his mother doesn't?"

"You call him a name like that and you want respect?" she said, getting her wind back. "He sees you sitting around here all day, milking a hurt foot for all it's worth. I haven't seen you limp once today."

"Not gonna be able to cover up your crime spree fast enough if I have to drag my leg everywhere I go," he shot back. "Fact is, you'd be nothing without me. You'd have been screwed today, that's for sure. You need a man around the house."

"That'd be nice," she said. "You know where I could find one?"

He lunged again, but before he could get his hands on her, she clawed his face. Raked her right hand down his left cheek, drawing blood.

"Motherfucker!" he said, jumping back. He put his hand to his cheek, looked at the blood on his palm. "Have you lost your mind?"

"You have to go back," Keisha said.

"Huh?"

"You have to go back and get that bag."

He shook his head. "No way."

She kept her voice low, so he'd have to listen. "If they open that bag and see what's inside, and remember my car, we're toast. You get that?"

Kirk grinned stupidly. "Not me, baby. You're the one whose ass is gonna fry."

"You think so? Wasn't me driving, wasn't me trying to get rid of evidence."

He looked at her, thinking it through, the grin fading. It took a few seconds. Like trying to explain the second law of thermonuclear dynamics to a pit bull, Keisha thought. "Shit," he said finally.

"You gotta get that bag. You gotta find out if they threw it in the Dumpster. And if they did, you gotta get rid of it someplace else."

"Oh, man," he said, almost pitiably. "I can't go back there."

"You *have* to," Keisha said. God, what a day and it was barely half over.

"Okay, okay," he said, accepting, at last, what he was going to have to do.

Should she tell him about the other problem? He

wasn't going to like it, but he was in this with her, like it or not.

"There's another thing," Keisha said.

He gave her a look that said *You're kiddin', right?*

"Garfield had one of my cards on him when he died. Sooner or later, the cops are going to show up and—"

Someone started banging on the door.

TWENTY-THREE

Rona Wedmore, sitting in the front seat of her unmarked car, put in a call to Joy from the forensics team.

"Hey," Joy said.

"Got your text. What's up?"

"We've only just removed the body, haven't gotten that far with it, except to tell you that needle went about five inches into the deceased's skull."

"You guessing that's what killed him?" Rona asked.

"You're funny," Joy said.

"I'm just asking, was there anything else done to him before that?"

"Don't think so, but you'll be the first to know what I find. Reason I called is, I got a look at the business card that was in his shirt. The name is . . . hang on, I wrote it down. Okay, 'Keisha Ceylon, Psychic Finder of Lost Souls.' Pretty classy." She read off a phone number and a website address, which Rona scribbled into her notebook.

"That name rings a bell," Rona said.

"Maybe you know her from another life," Joy said.

"You remember that case, it's got to be five or six years ago now, about the Milford woman whose family disappeared when she was fourteen? She went something like twenty-five years not knowing what happened to them."

"Archer," Joy said. "Cynthia Archer. At the time, I kept thinking, why couldn't that happen to my family?"

"This Keisha woman's name came up back then." Wedmore thought about it. "Claimed to have visions about people who vanish. I think she tried to shake down the Archers."

"I'm going to hand over all matters related to visions to you," Joy said. "There's something else. Looks like footprints just outside the side living room window, in the flower beds. Ground wasn't that frozen. And there may be some prints on the glass."

Wedmore didn't know what to make of that, but asked to be kept posted.

Once she was done talking to Joy, the detective made several other calls from her cell. When she'd gotten the answers to some questions that were on her mind, she keyed the ignition and drove to Old Fairfield High School.

She went straight to the office, identified herself to the secretaries at the counter, and said she needed to speak to a member of their staff. "Just ask him to come down here. Don't mention who it is."

One of the secretaries consulted a timetable on her computer screen. "But he's teaching American Literature right now." Wedmore gave her a look that seemed to ask whether the study of Ralph Waldo Emerson or Herman Melville trumped her request.

The secretary picked up the phone, got the person she was looking for, and delivered the message. Wedmore commandeered a small empty room—the guidance counselor's officer, as it turned out—and waited.

Three minutes later, Terry Archer walked in. When he saw who was waiting for him, his face fell.

"Oh my God," he said. "What's happened?"

Wedmore flashed him a reassuring smile. "Nothing, Mr. Archer, nothing." She extended a hand and the teacher took it, but he looked far from comforted. "It's good to see you," she said.

"I'd like to say the same," Archer said. "But seeing you, it's given me something of a start. You're sure everything's okay? Is Grace okay? Is this about Cynthia?"

"So far as I know, your daughter and wife are perfectly fine. I'm not here about them. How are they, anyway?"

Archer offered up a pained smile. "Grace is good."

"I remember she had a real thing for astronomy. Is she still into that?"

Archer nodded. "She wants to be an astronaut. Wants to get a little closer to the stars. She's pretty upset they've mothballed the space shuttle."

Wedmore grinned. "Well, I'm sure they'll get around to going back to space at some point. And Mrs. Archer—Cynthia. How's she doing?"

Archer hesitated. "She's good. She's okay."

Wedmore knew there was something going on, so she said nothing, waited for Archer to volunteer more information.

"It's been hard for her," Archer said. "Getting the answers to what happened to her family, it didn't . . . it's not like it made everything perfect. Sometimes, getting your questions answered, it just raises new ones. Like, how do I move on, knowing what I know? Right now, Cyn's kind of taking some time to herself."

"You're separated?"

He shook his head. "No, no, not that. Not exactly. But she needs a bit of space at the moment. Grace is with me." He shrugged. "Things'll work out. You know, one way or another. They have to."

"I'm sorry," Wedmore said. "How's Grace been handling it?"

"Well, she's getting into those teen years, you know? It's hard to know what she's thinking. She doesn't like to let me in." He shrugged. "But I guess every parent of a teenage girl goes through that, right?"

Wedmore waved her hand around the room. "When I started calling around, I didn't think you were still teaching here."

"I transferred back a couple of years ago," Archer said. "But it was good, taking some time away from this place. Listen, I got a class of aspiring first of-fenders who'd rather steal shopping carts than hear about Hemingway, so if there's something I can help you—"

"Keisha Ceylon," Wedmore said.

"Jesus."

"That got a reaction. What can you tell me about her?"

"After they did that TV show, about it being twenty-five years since Cynthia's parents and her brother disappeared, that woman came out of the woodwork, claiming she knew things about the case. Not first-hand knowledge, but things she'd seen in a dream or a vision or something. Cynthia and I were asked to come down to the TV station for a follow-up, so this so-called psychic could tell us on camera what she knew, but when she found out the station wasn't giving her a thousand bucks, she clammed up."

"Hmm," said Wedmore.

"She came by the house one other time, trying to shake us down personally. Cynthia threw her out on her ass."

"Has she ever been in touch since?"

Archer shook his head. "Never heard from her again."

"What was your sense of her?" Wedmore asked.

A small shrug. "Two short meetings, that was it. But she was an opportunist. She liked to take advantage of people when they were at their most vulnerable. That puts her pretty high on my list of lowlifes."

Wedmore smiled. "Yeah, I can see that."

"Is she still out there, doing her thing?"

"Maybe."

Something flashed in Archer's eyes and his brow furrowed. "That thing on the news. The man and his daughter. Asking for information about his wife."

Wedmore nodded and extended her hand again. "Thank you for your help. I should let you get back to your students."

Archer tried to smile one last time, but Wedmore could sense the effort. The man wore his sadness like a jacket. "Actually, it is nice to see you again. You were a great help to us at a very dark time."

He slipped out of the guidance counselor's office. Wedmore had a strange feeling, as she watched him leave, that she would see him again before long.

TWENTY-FOUR

"Shit," Keisha said as the banging on the door continued.

"What are you gonna do?" Kirk said, dabbing blood from his cheek with a tissue.

Keisha stood there, frozen, not sure whether to answer it, or escape out the back door and jump the neighbour's fence. The latter seemed like a pretty stupid idea. If this was the cops wanting to talk to her, they probably already had someone covering the back door.

"I've got no choice," she said, took a breath, and opened the door.

"Oh, thank God you're home!" said Gail Beaudry, who had her hand raised, ready to knock again. The woman's eyes were bloodshot from crying.

"Gail?" Keisha said.

"I *have* to talk to you!" the woman said, forcing her way into Keisha's house. She glanced at Kirk, who was standing there, dumbfounded. "I have to talk to you *alone.*"

"This isn't a good time," Keisha said. "Maybe later this week, but right now—"

"He's dead!" Gail blurted. "My brother's dead."

"What?"

"Someone killed my brother!"

"Gail, I don't know what you're talking about."

"This morning," she said. "And they're saying all these horrible things about Melissa. Ridiculous things! That she killed her mother. It's all crazy. The police have everything all wrong! You have to help me! You have to make them see the truth!"

Keisha was getting a very bad feeling. She grabbed Gail by the shoulders, steadied her and looked into her eyes. "Gail, stop, just *stop* for a second. Who's your brother?"

"Wendell," she said. "Wendell Garfield."

Keisha exchanged a look with Kirk, who was standing to Gail's side. He mouthed, "What the fuck?"

"Okay, Gail, come sit down and tell me all about this. Do you want something to drink? Kirk, get her something to drink."

"Do you have anything diet?" Gail asked, allowing Keisha to lead her to the couch.

"Just get something," Keisha said, sitting down next to Gail, knees touching. She was massaging the woman's shoulder comfortingly. "It's going to be okay. You just need to tell me what's happened, but slowly, from the start."

Kirk handed Gail a can of Diet Pepsi that he'd already cracked open. Gail looked at him and said, "What happened to your face?"

"Shaving," he said.

She nodded, then answered Keisha's question. "A few days ago, Ellie, that's Wendell's wife, she disappeared."

"I saw something on the news about that," Keisha said.

Gail nodded. "They held a press conference and everything yesterday. Wendell and Melissa. Oh, God." She set the can of Pepsi on the table and put her hands over her eyes. "It's all so unbelievable! Why would they hold the press conference if Melissa had something to do with it?"

"Gail, so what are you saying? It was the *daughter*?" As soon as she said it, Keisha realized how it might sound; that she was surprised that *Wendell* wasn't the one responsible. She had to recalibrate her thinking, to act surprised by everything she was about to hear, to listen and react without preconceptions.

In fact, she wouldn't have to try all that hard.

"That's what they're saying," Gail said, shaking her head. "That Melissa killed her mother."

Keisha tried to get her head around that. If Melissa had killed Ellie Garfield, why had the husband tried to strangle her? He must have been in on it, or at the very least, been helping his daughter cover up after the fact.

"And what exactly happened to Wendell?" Keisha asked. "Where did they find him?"

"At home," Gail said. "I don't really know all the details. But none of this makes any sense. That Melissa would kill her mother, that someone would kill Wendell. It's insane."

Keisha put her arms around Gail. "You poor thing. This is so horrible for you."

As she held the woman, Keisha's mind raced.

Once Kirk finally disposed of the bloody clothes, the only thing that connected her to Garfield was the business card she was sure the police would find. She'd convinced herself she could explain that away by saying there were a hundred places Garfield could have picked one up.

But now there was a definite link between Keisha and the dead man.

The dead man's sister. Who just happened to be one of Keisha's clients.

Not good, not good at—

But wait a second.

Maybe there was an opportunity here.

"Tell me about your brother," Keisha said. "Was he older, younger?"

"He was my *baby* brother," she said, and began to weep again.

"I think—haven't you mentioned him in some of our sessions?"

She nodded, grabbed a couple of tissues from the box on the table, which was right next to the unfinished Twinkie and beer, and blew her nose. Then she had a sip of her Pepsi, and said, "That's right. I mentioned a few times to him that I came to see you, that you helped me to connect with my past lives."

"What did he think of that?"

"Oh, he was very dismissive, but no more than my husband. Jerry thinks I'm a total crackpot." She managed a short laugh. "Maybe I am."

"No, not at all," Keisha said. "Everyone has different things they believe in. They're coping strategies.

They help us deal with the world out there. Was Wendell dealing with a lot of things? Difficult things?"

"Oh, my, yes. Melissa's been a constant source of stress for him and Ellie. She—oh, I can't believe Ellie's actually dead too. Melissa left home at sixteen, lived on her own, then met this man who got her pregnant. Ellie and Wendell were worried sick about her."

"Did you try to offer advice to them? Give them any suggestions? I mean, you're Melissa's aunt. I could imagine you wanted to help them where you could."

"Of course, of course, I tried."

"Is that why you took my card?" Keisha said. This was either going to work or it wasn't. "To give it to your brother and his wife? In case they ever wanted to consult with me? Because, given what you've said about him, it seems unlikely he'd have been in touch."

Gail pulled away from Keisha's embrace. "Did I do that?"

"You don't remember?"

Gail blinked a couple of times. "I don't . . . I'm not sure."

"It was some time ago. You know that period where you believed you were channeling Amelia Earhart?"

Gail nodded. "That was a couple of years ago."

"I think it was while you were talking as Amelia

that you asked me for a card. You said you had someone you thought I could help."

Gail was still trying to recall. "That's possible. I think I remember. Maybe I was thinking of giving it to Ellie. She probably wouldn't have believed in what you do any more than Wendell, but at least she wasn't totally closed-minded."

Keisha liked the way this was going. Gail, like so many of Keisha's regulars, was very suggestible.

"So you must have given it to your brother or your sister-in-law at some point, or else one of them saw the card at your place and helped themselves to it." Keisha waved her hand as though it didn't matter. "But what I need to know is, what can I do for you, right now? How can I help you through this?"

"I knew you'd be here for me," Gail said. "I tried Jerry's phone after I tried calling you." That must have been when the phone rang earlier, Keisha thought. "But his went to voicemail, and the truth is, I didn't really want to talk to him anyway. He's never been there for me the way you have."

For fifty dollars an hour.

Keisha hugged her again. "I just want you to know that any time you need to come by and talk, it's okay."

Gail smiled and dabbed her eyes again. "There is something. And I'd certainly be willing to pay you for your time, more than your usual rate."

Keisha said, hesitantly, "Well, Gail, like I said, any time you want to talk . . ."

"No, I need you for more than that. You see, Keisha, the police don't know what they're doing.

They have Melissa in custody for something she couldn't possibly have done. And if they've got that all wrong, I know they're going to get the investigation into my brother's death all mixed up too."

"I don't really know what I could—"

"I want you to help me. I want you to help me find out who killed Wendell, and what really happened to Ellie."

"Gail, I'm not a detective," Keisha protested.

"I know!" she said. "That's what makes you the perfect person to help. You see things no one else can. I'll bet you—I'll bet you if you came with me to my brother's house, you could just *tell* what happened. Remember that story you told me, about the little girl who was abducted and was in the neighbor's house, with all the sports trophies around her? You *solved* that! If you hadn't had that vision, that girl would be dead now. You told me that yourself."

Keisha disentangled herself from Gail Beaudry and stood up. "I might have embellished that story just a little bit."

Gail slapped Keisha's hand. "You're just being modest. I know what you can do."

"But I really don't think I could help you here. I mean, the police aren't going to want me sticking my nose into this. They have a thing about mediums and psychics. They think we're crazy."

Gail stood defiantly. "I don't care what they say. If you're working for me, there's nothing they can do about it."

Keisha looked at Kirk. She couldn't read what

was on his face, which was still bloodied from when she scratched him. Maybe he was too stupefied to register anything.

All Keisha knew was, she could not go back to that house.

She believed she'd successfully planted the seed with Gail about her business card, and that when the police finally came around to ask about it, she had a plausible explanation for how it ended up in Wendell Garfield's pocket without her ever being at his house. He'd come upon the card, maybe in a drawer, and hung onto it, thinking he might work up the nerve to call Keisha to help him find his wife.

Except it was clear from what Gail had told her that Garfield knew what had happened to his wife. His daughter had killed her, and he'd helped her cover her tracks. So why would he need a psychic's help?

But he and Melissa had held a press conference seeking information from the public when they really didn't need it. So wasn't it plausible that Garfield might engage a medium to maintain the fiction that he didn't know what had happened to his—

"I'll pay you five thousand dollars," Gail said.

"What?" Keisha said.

"I'll pay you five thousand dollars to help me with this, to get to the truth."

Keisha shook her head, "I don't know, Gail. I—"

"She'll do it," Kirk said.

TWENTY-FIVE

"Can I talk to you for a second?" Keisha said to Kirk, drawing him into the kitchen while Gail Beaudry stayed in the living room.

"Are you crazy?" she whispered to him once they were out of earshot.

"It's five grand," he said. "Just don't go into the house and go all weird and say holy shit, I think *I* did it."

"I can't go into that house. Not again."

"Sure you can," he said. "Might as well make something out of this fucked-up day." Kirk didn't know she'd actually gotten some cash out of Garfield before things went off the rails. But even if he did, he'd still want her to go after this. Five thousand was a lot of money.

"It's wrong," Keisha said. "You don't see something wrong, taking this woman's money to help her figure out who killed her brother? You don't see something just a bit off with that?"

Kirk shrugged. "So? Like you've never faked this stuff before?"

"I can't do this, I—"

"Is everything okay?" Gail asked. She was standing in the kitchen doorway.

"Yes," Kirk said. "Keisha was just saying, she hates

to ask you at a time like this, but she needs her fee up front, in cash."

Gail's eyes popped for a second, but she said, "We can stop at the bank on the way to my brother's house. Would that be okay?"

"That'd be fine," Kirk said.

Keisha struggled to focus. She said to Gail, "Why don't you wait in the car and I'll be right out."

Once the door was closed, Kirk said, "This lady has to be loaded. I bet you can get even more out of her. Where's she get all the dough?"

Keisha shook her head, like this was not uppermost in her mind, but said, "Her husband's in real estate and she inherited some fortune when her parents died. I don't care if she's married to Bill Gates, I'm not going to milk this beyond the five grand."

Kirk gave her a disapproving look.

"And you," she said, "have to go back and find out what happened to that bag."

"Yeah, yeah, I hear ya."

Keisha glanced at the wall clock. "I don't know how long I'm going to be with her. You have to be back here for when Matthew gets home."

"Why? He's got his own key. Since when do I—"

"What if the police are here? I don't want him coming home, finding a cop on the doorstep. He'll be scared to death, thinking something has happened to me."

Kirk sighed. "Fine, I'll be here. But you're really turning him into a momma's boy."

★

Keisha got in Gail Beaudry's Jaguar. The woman talked non-stop all the way to her bank in downtown Milford, on the green.

"I don't know why they have Melissa in custody or why they think she had anything to do with this. They say she confessed, but that's ridiculous. Why would a girl kill her own mother? That's absolutely unthinkable. I don't understand how something like that could happen. Maybe if it were an accident, like if she'd backed into her with her car, didn't know she was there, but to deliberately do it? That defies belief. I know that girl was a world of trouble to her mother, but deep down she loved her very much. I just know that."

Keisha wondered whether she was going to be sick again. Any second now, she might have to ask Gail to pull to the side of the road.

Since killing Garfield, she'd devoted all of her energy to covering her tracks. Going back for the earring, disposing of her clothes (a problem she hoped would soon be resolved), standing in the shower until the water ran cold, getting Kirk to clean her car. And after an initial panic about her business card, she'd come up with a creative solution involving Gail that she believed could withstand scrutiny.

But having made all these efforts to distance herself from the event, here she was, sitting in this car, heading back to the crime scene.

"I'll just bet the police put Melissa in a room and browbeat her with questions and that was how they made her confess to something she never did," Gail continued. "That's what the police do. We think that kind of thing only happens in Russia or China or Latin American countries, but it happens right here in the good ol' USA, don't you kid yourself. The police just want to close cases. It doesn't matter to them whether they've got the right person or not. And I don't even know what happened to Ellie. If they're charging Melissa, what is it exactly they think she did to her mother? And what does it have to do with Wendell. I'm telling you—"

"Please stop," Keisha said.

"What?"

"I . . . I need to concentrate."

"Of course, of course you do. I'm so sorry. Here we are anyway. I'll go in and get your money." Gail left the motor running as she got out of the car and went into the bank.

Take the car and run, Keisha thought. *Or leave the car, but still run.*

But where would she go? How far could she get? How long would it take for the police to find her? And if she wasn't already a suspect, wouldn't running change that? And how could she even think of leaving Matthew behind?

She'd never do that. Keisha was a lot of things— and she knew it—but she was not the kind of mother who'd abandon her child.

I could take him with me.

Sure, that was a plan. Go on the run with a kid. Keisha told herself to stop it. She was in this up to her eyeballs now, and she was going to have to see how things played out.

Gail returned in five minutes, clutching a plain white banking envelope, the kind used for deposits at the ATMs. She got in the car and handed the envelope to Keisha.

"There you go," she said, doing up her seat belt. "Good thing I have my own account. Jerry would have an absolute heart attack if he knew I was doing this."

"Thank you," Keisha said, putting the envelope into her purse. She'd had to grab one of her other ones as she was leaving, and toss her wallet into it.

"You don't want to count it?"

"I trust you," Keisha said.

That made Gail Beaudry smile. She reached over and touched Keisha's arm. "I trust you, too. I want to thank you for helping me."

Keisha couldn't look at her.

"Let's go over to Wendell's house now and see if any of the police there will tell us what's going on. Maybe, as we get close, you'll start picking up some signals or something," Gail said.

They could see police cars as soon as Gail turned onto the street. Cruisers had been used to block off the street in both directions about a hundred feet each side of the house. Gail pulled the Jag over to the shoulder and said, "Watch your step. It looks slippery here."

They came around the front of the car and approached the house together. As they started walking up the driveway, a female uniformed officer came down to meet them.

"Can I help you?" she asked.

Gail said, "I'm Mrs. Beaudry, and this is my associate. We'd like to speak to whoever's in charge here. Is that you?"

"No, ma'am. What's your interest here?"

"This is my brother's house. Wendell Garfield. The man who was killed."

The officer nodded. "If you'll wait here, I'll see what I can do." Keisha watched her go into the house and close the door.

Don't want to go in there.

Gail stood with her arms crossed. After a couple of minutes, she said, "This is what they do. They keep you waiting to wear you down. It's all part of the game they play."

Keisha thought that if anyone was playing a game, it was herself.

The officer came back out of the house and told them she had reached the detective in charge of the investigation, and she'd be coming by shortly.

"Would that be that black woman?" Gail asked. "Wedmore?"

"Yes."

"Fine, but can we wait in the house, where it's warmer?"

"I'm sorry, no, you can't come in. Not without Detective Wedmore's approval."

"We'll be in the car, then," Gail said, and the two of them turned to start walking back to it. They were just about to open the doors when an unmarked car pulled up and Rona Wedmore got out.

She recognized the dead man's sister from their meeting at the station. "Hello, Mrs. Beaudry."

"I want some answers," Gail said. "I want some answers right now."

Wedmore cast an eye at Keisha, then looked back at Gail. "What would you like to know?"

"What happened to my brother?"

Wedmore's gaze turned back to Keisha. "Who are you?"

"I'm Keisha Ceylon."

The corners of the detective's mouth turned up. "I was just talking to someone who knows you."

TWENTY-SIX

"Excuse me?" Keisha said.

"Terry Archer," Wedmore said, giving Keisha a knowing look. "You offered to help him and his wife a few years back."

"I remember," Keisha said. "If Mr. Archer says he knows me, that's not true. We met twice, very briefly."

"Fair enough. But you certainly made an impression."

Don't be evasive, Keisha thought. Don't be defensive. Tackle this head on. "I'm sure. I offered to help him and his wife when they were having their troubles and they chose not to engage me. Mr. Archer, in particular, was very skeptical of my gifts. All I wanted to do was help them."

Wedmore nodded. Before she could reply, Gail said, "I've engaged Ms Ceylon to help *me*. Clearly you already know her, but if you're thinking she's here to help you, she's not. She's representing my interests. All you people care about is making sure someone gets charged, whether it's the right person or not. Do you know who did this to my brother?"

"We're in the early stages of the investigation," Wedmore said patiently.

"Are you still holding Melissa?"

"We are."

"That's ridiculous. You *have* to release her. Imagine what she's going through. Losing her mother, and then her father, all within a few days. And suggesting she confessed! What on earth would she confess to? And where *is* Ellie? What's happened to her body? Are you telling me Melissa was able to make her mother's body disappear?"

Tiredly, Wedmore said, "We can set up a meeting between you and Melissa. From what I can see, you're the only family she has left. She waived her right to legal representation, but you should get her to rethink that, so she gets the best advice possible as this moves forward. There may be extenuating circumstances that might have an impact on sentencing. You might want—"

"Good heavens, what on earth did she tell you?"

Wedmore sighed. "Melissa stabbed her mother, called her father, and he helped her cover it up. They drove the car out onto a lake and waited for it to go through the ice."

Wow, Keisha thought. *Maybe I really* can *do this.*

Gail was speechless, so Wedmore added, "What we're trying to figure out now is what kind of connection there may be between Ellie's death, and what happened to your brother."

Gail managed to ask, "Is my brother's body still in the house?"

"No. The coroner is conducting a post-mortem."

"Ms Ceylon wants to go inside."

"Excuse me?" said Wedmore.

"No," Keisha protested. "That's not nece—"

"She needs to go inside and see what she can feel," Gail said. She looked at Keisha and said, "I'm betting the sooner you get in, the better, right? The vibrations, whatever it is you feel, will still be fresh?"

"It may already be too late," Keisha said.

Gail took hold of Keisha's arm and looked imploringly at her. "I know it's a lot to ask, but I can't do it. I can't go in there. I want you to be my eyes. I want you to see where it happened. Won't that help you? Won't that help you visualize, to connect, to feel what happened?"

Keisha said, "If you could just find something of your brother's for me. Maybe you have a letter at home from him."

Gail continued to squeeze her arm. "I really need you to do this." She turned to Wedmore and pleaded, "Will you allow her to see where it happened?"

Wedmore thought for a moment. "Ordinarily, I'd say no, but I think maybe it'd be a good idea for Ms Ceylon to come in and have a look-see."

Keisha was taken aback. She couldn't see Wedmore playing along with this unless there was something in it for her. "I totally understand if you'd rather I stayed out here and—"

"Come on," said Wedmore. "Mrs. Beaudry, why don't you wait in your car and stay warm while we do this?"

"All right," she said, as Wedmore put her hand gently on Keisha's back and led her toward the house.

She took her hand away as they continued walking. "How did you and Mrs. Beaudry connect?"

"She's a client of mine," Keisha said. "She's consulted me for a few years now."

"What kind of consulting?"

"You'd have to ask her that."

"Oh. Psychic–client privilege?"

Keisha gave Wedmore a look. "That's why I don't come to the police when I have information about a crime."

"Information? What do you mean by information?"

"Things come to me, Detective. Visions, images, like pieces of a puzzle. But I don't expect you to believe me any more than the Archers did."

"When we go into the house, you're not to touch anything. And we're just going to step in. You can see the living room from the front door."

"Is that where it happened?" Keisha asked.

Wedmore looked at her and smiled. "Yes, that's where it happened." The officer Keisha and Gail had spoken to earlier was guarding the front door, and stepped aside to let them through.

Keisha was rehearsing in her head how she'd act surprised. Turned out she didn't need to rehearse at all.

What she saw as she looked into the living room horrified her.

A massive puddle of dark red had saturated the broadloom. It was concentrated in one area, but there were scattered splotches of red between where the body had been and the door.

"Dear God," Keisha said, her eyes fixed on the scene for several seconds before she turned away. "That's horrible."

"Yes," said Wedmore. "It's pretty bad."

"Can we go now?"

"Let's just hang in for a second. Give your spidey senses a chance to pick something up, see who did it."

Keisha shot her a look, and turned away from the living room. "It's not like that. I can't just say, oh, it was a man, six two, heavyset, with a thick beard and a dark coat, driving a red Mustang, license plate 459J87."

"Is that a vision that just came to you?"

"No! I'm trying to make a point."

"Okay, okay," said Wedmore. "Maybe it would help, though, if you looked into the room one more time. There's some things I could point out to you."

"Like what?"

"Pull yourself together and have a look."

Keisha did as she was told, steeled herself, and turned around. "What things?"

"You see the pink robe over there?"

"Yes."

"And if you look there, you'll see the sash from the robe. Also pink."

"Okay."

"So why isn't the sash in the loops of the robe, do you think?"

Keisha resisted an urge to touch her neck. "I don't know. Do you?"

"No. But I've an idea. I'm wondering if there was an attempted strangulation."

"Oh."

"Yeah. I've been trying to think it through. You see, I don't think anyone came here intending to kill Mr. Garfield. I mean, if you were coming here to kill him, you'd bring along something other than a knitting needle, don't you think?"

"A knitting needle?" Keisha said. "He was killed with a knitting needle?"

Wedmore nodded. "That's right. If you were coming here intending to kill him, you'd bring a gun, or a knife, even a baseball bat. Wouldn't you?"

"I don't know," Keisha said.

"To kill him with a knitting needle, that tells me that the perpetrator acted impulsively, that the needle was the closest thing at hand."

"You may be right, I honestly have no idea. Do I have to keep looking?"

Wedmore ignored the question. "Even then, if you were going to act, like I said, impulsively, wouldn't you be more likely to just hit him? Or grab something in the room that's heavy and clunk him over the head with that? Like a lamp, or an ashtray, maybe, although I don't think Mr. Garfield smoked."

"Really, I have no idea."

"To my way of thinking, the knitting needle is an act of desperation. A last-ditch effort or attempt at something. Maybe the only thing that the person who did this could reach. I'm even thinking it might have been a defensive move."

"Defensive?" Keisha asked.

"Now we're back to the sash. Suppose Mr. Garfield was strangling someone with that, and that someone grabbed the needle to try to save himself."

"You know it was a man?" Keisha asked.

"I'm just saying," Wedmore said. "I think it could as easily have been a woman."

Keisha swallowed but said nothing.

"Is that how it happened?" Wedmore asked.

"I don't know," Keisha said. "I'm not picking up anything like that."

"No, no," Wedmore said. "I don't mean in a vision. Is that how it happened, to you?"

"What?"

"Did he try to strangle you, Ms Ceylon? When you came here to offer your services? Did he think you knew what had happened?"

Keisha stared, dumbfounded, at Wedmore. "What?"

"I was wondering if that's how it played out," the detective said innocently.

"I have absolutely no idea what you're talking about. I've never been here before."

"You're sure about that?"

"I am."

"Because we found your card. Tucked right into Mr. Garfield's shirt pocket. Your card, Ms Ceylon. With your name on it, your phone number and website. 'Finder of Lost Souls,' it said on it."

"Really? He had my card?"

"How do you explain that?"

"Well, I mean, quite easily, actually."

Wedmore raised her eyebrows. "Go ahead."

"I've provided business cards in the past to Gail, to Mrs. Beaudry. She must have given one to her brother. You should ask her about it."

"I will."

"And when he started wondering whether you were ever going to find his wife, he went looking for that card and was probably going to give me a call."

"You were paying attention outside, weren't you?" Wedmore asked.

"About what?"

"Wendell Garfield knew what had happened to his wife. He helped get rid of her body. He hardly needed to engage the services of a psychic to find her."

"It makes about as much sense to call me as to call a press conference," Keisha shot back.

Wedmore smiled. "Yes, but that was a performance. A public demonstration to make us think he and his daughter were in the dark about what happened to Ellie Garfield. But one of your cards, tucked into his shirt? Who was he trying to impress with that?"

Keisha said nothing.

"You know what I think?" Wedmore said. "I think you came here and tried the same scam you tried with the Archers. Asked Garfield for money in exchange for information you really didn't have. It's your thing. It's what you do. And then something

226

went wrong. I don't know what, exactly. But he ended up dead, and you got away."

"That's insane," Keisha said, feeling as though her insides would let loose. "I can't take any more of this. I'm leaving."

She was turning for the door when Wedmore reached out and held her arm. "I've a card of my own I'd like to give you." She placed it in Keisha's palm. "You find yourself changing your mind, wanting to talk, you call me any time."

"I think that's unlikely," Keisha said, pulling her arm away and heading outside, but tucking the card into her coat pocket.

She was a few steps down the walk when Wedmore called to her. "That high collar you're wearing, it's the perfect thing when it's cold like this, isn't it?"

TWENTY-SEVEN

Kirk figured it made more sense to take his pickup this time. Those two guys from the pizza place would recognize Keisha's car, not that he was planning to drive right up to the Dumpster this time anyway.

He wasn't an idiot.

He remembered there was another small strip of stores just past the one with the pizza place, to the north. He figured on parking there and then back-tracking, grabbing the right bag, then getting the hell home.

It didn't take him more than fifteen minutes to return. He wheeled the pickup into the next business lot, a place that made and sold metal fasteners, pulling in between a couple of other trucks. The lot was nearly full, which was good. Kirk didn't believe anyone was going to notice if he left his pickup here for a few minutes.

He got out and walked down the alley—wide enough for a good-sized truck—between the two buildings. At the rear, the properties weren't sep-arated by a formal fence, but there was a thicket of bushes and rubbish that kept Kirk from strolling directly to the Dumpster behind the pizza place.

He'd considered waiting until it was dark to do this, but there was no one around, so he used his arms to part a way through the bushes toward the neighboring property. He was about forty feet from the Dumpster. The bag he'd left behind wasn't on the pavement, so unless those two clowns had decided to take it inside and open it up, odds were they'd just tossed it into the bin after he'd sped off. What else where they going to do with it? Would they really be pissed off enough to go through the contents of the bag, looking for discarded bills or receipts, hoping to find an address? Did working at a pizza place pay enough to make you have to do that kind of shit?

Kirk doubted it.

But even if they'd tossed the bag into the Dumpster and forgotten about it, Kirk supposed he could see why Keisha had her panties in a knot about getting it out of there and dumping it someplace else. If there ever was a news story about someone trying to dispose of evidence in the Garfield killing, these guys might remember his visit, put it together, put in a call to the cops.

And if the trash hadn't been collected by then . . .

So maybe, sometimes, Keisha was right. But not always. If it hadn't been for him speaking up, she'd have turned down a chance to make an easy five grand. If that Beaudry woman wanted to throw money at Keisha, she should take it. Okay, he could see why the whole thing would make her a little squeamish, but for that kind of money she needed to suck it up. All she had to do was what she always did. Spin out enough bullshit to get the client engaged, make them think they were getting their money's worth.

Piece of cake.

The way Kirk figured it, if there was anyone putting himself at risk in this operation, it was him. Out here in the freezing cold, huddling in the bushes, waiting for a chance to do a Dumpster dive.

Kirk emerged from the bushes and was almost to the car-sized rectangular bin when he saw the back door to the pizza place swing open. He hunched down and scurried in behind the Dumpster, out of sight.

He heard the door close, but didn't know if that meant someone had stepped out, or gone back inside. He crept to the edge of the bin and dared to peek around.

It was the second man he'd encountered, the big white guy. He was standing there, a couple of feet beyond the door, the cold misting his breath. No, wait, he was on a smoke break.

The man hadn't slipped on a jacket, so Kirk didn't think he'd stand out there all that long. Frostbite trumped nicotine addiction, right? He'd get enough of a fix, then head back in.

But the guy kept standing there. Then he turned, looking in Kirk's direction.

Shit.

Kirk, on his hands and knees, edged back from the corner of the Dumpster. He wasn't wearing gloves, and the thin layer of nearly melted snow was cold on his bare palms and soaking through the knees of his jeans. He stayed crouched down like that, and tried to hold his frosty breath as long as he could.

He heard whistling. The pizza guy was having a smoke and a whistle. Kirk was trying to place the tune, but the man was a weak, off-key whistler, so it took a few seconds before Kirk realized he was attempting "The Long and Winding Road". *Yeah,* Kirk thought. *That's what I feel like I'm on. This is one motherfucking crazy day and it can't come to an end soon enough.*

The whistling grew more faint. It sounded as though the man was strolling back toward the building. Then Kirk heard the door open, and, half a second later, slam shut.

He crawled to the edge of the Dumpster and peered around. There was no one there.

He wondered whether the big man's buddy smoked too, and if he did, whether they took their smoke breaks in shifts. Which would mean the other guy might walk out that door any second.

Kirk had to move quickly.

He got up on his feet and came around the front of the Dumpster. He worked the heel of his left hand under the lid and pushed up, then leaned his head over the edge. The first thing his eyes landed on was a garbage bag with a red drawstring tie. He reached in with his free hand, grabbed the top end of the bag, made a fist around it, and twisted it around his wrist.

He drew out the bag, let the lid down gently so it wouldn't make a huge racket, slipped back through the bushes without catching the plastic bag on any of the sharp branches, and was back to his truck in under a minute.

The outside of the bag wasn't as clean as it had been when he'd left Keisha's house with it. Scraps of pizza, spilled pop, all kinds of sticky shit. He sure as hell wasn't going to put it up front in the cab with him. He didn't even like the idea of dropping it into the cargo bed, but there wasn't much he could do about that.

Kirk got in the truck, keyed the ignition, and happened to look down at the dashboard clock. It was nearly half past three.

Son of a bitch. The li'l fucker could be home in ten minutes, if he didn't stop off at a friend's house or get beat up on the way home. Kirk didn't think he needed to be there for him, but he supposed Keisha was right. If he came home and the police were there, and his mom wasn't, he'd probably go off on a crying jag. But chances were, the cops wouldn't be there. If they came by and no one was home, they'd take off and come back later. Kirk decided to grab the kid, offer to take him to the food court at the Post Mall, and pitch the bag in one of the garbage bins there.

He backed out of the spot, threw the truck into drive, and nearly cut off a woman in a Lexus SUV as he swerved back onto the road with a screech.

About a half-mile later, he glanced into the rear-view mirror, checking not only for traffic, but the bag.

Didn't see it.

"Jesus!" he shouted. "No way! No fucking way!"

He wheeled the car onto the shoulder and slammed the brakes. He jumped out the door and looked into the cargo bed, his heart pounding.

The bag was there. It had worked its way up to the front, right under the cab window.

Kirk closed his eyes for a second, breathed a sigh of relief, got back into the truck and continued on.

TWENTY-EIGHT

Gail Beaudry got out of her Jaguar as Keisha approached.

"What did you see? Do you know who did it? What happened?"

Keisha waved at her to get back in the car. She came around the passenger side and got in herself.

She was shaking.

"What?" Gail asked. "You look terrible. Did you see something? I mean in your head, did you see what actually happened?"

"Please, Gail, I need a second," Keisha said, holding up her hand.

"Of course, of course, I totally understand. I know these things you see, it's not like you can turn them on and off like they're a DVD or—"

"Shut up!" Keisha exploded. "Just shut up for a minute."

The way Gail recoiled, if the driver's door hadn't been there, she'd have fallen out of her seat. Her mouth was agape. She burst into tears.

"Gail," Keisha said, suddenly feeling sorry.

Gail had one hand over her eyes and the other, palm out, toward Keisha. She sobbed for a good half-minute before Keisha said, "Really, I'm sorry. It was just . . . so horrible in there."

Gail's attitude did a one-eighty. "Oh, of course. *I'm* the one who should be sorry. I made you go in there. I shouldn't have done it. It was too much to ask. I feel terrible." She held Keisha's arm.

"It's okay," Keisha said. She noticed Detective Wedmore walking down the Garfield driveway, pausing at the end, looking in their direction.

"I've probably traumatized you," Gail said. "It was wrong of me."

"It's okay. I just . . . I guess I didn't expect it to affect me the way it did."

What Keisha hadn't expected was how quickly Wedmore was putting it together. All because of that damn business card. But she had that covered, right?

"Did you . . . did you sense anything?"

Keisha looked down into her lap and shook her head a couple of times. "Not really."

"Maybe it'll come to you later?"

She looked at Gail, saw the wanting in her eyes, the *hope*.

"The police may be able to figure this one out before I can," Keisha said.

"I don't trust them," Gail said. "I don't trust the police at all."

Keisha saw that Wedmore was walking toward them.

"There's lots of people you shouldn't trust," Keisha said. "Not just the police." She looked down at her purse, sitting on the floor between her feet. "I've been thinking, Gail, about this five thousand dollars you've given me. I don't know that I deserve—"

"That detective's coming this way," Gail said. "What do you think she wants?"

Keisha hated to think. "I don't know. But, Gail, about this money, I—"

"I don't like her," Gail said. "I don't like her one bit. And it's not because she's black. I have nothing against black people. But don't you think it's possible that, at some level, she likes sticking it to white people, whether they're guilty or not? A kind of way to get even?"

"I don't think so," Keisha said. She opened her purse and was about to reach in for the envelope stuffed with cash, but stopped when she heard tapping at Gail's window.

Gail powered it down.

"Yes, Detective?"

Wedmore said, "Mrs. Beaudry, I'd like to speak with you."

"Is this going to take long?"

"I don't know."

"Because I don't want to keep Ms Ceylon here. I'm driving her home."

Wedmore thought about that briefly, and flagged over one of the uniforms. Then she put her head half into the open window and said, "Ms Ceylon, that officer will give you a lift home. I don't want to see you inconvenienced."

"That's okay," Keisha said. "I don't mind waiting for Gail."

Wedmore said, firmly, "No, we'll give you a ride. Mrs. Beaudry?"

Gail sighed, powered up the window and turned off the engine. "We'll talk later, okay? Because maybe by then you'll know something."

No, I'm not going to know anything, Keisha thought. *I want to forget all of this*. She just wanted to give the woman her money back and never see her again. She'd very nearly done it, too.

Gail got out of the car. A Milford police cruiser pulled up. Wedmore spoke to the driver, then looked at Keisha and waited. Reluctantly, Keisha moved from the Jag to the police car, Wedmore holding the door for her, saying, "I'll drop by and see you a little later."

Keisha felt the dread envelop her like a cold, wet sleeping bag.

Kirk's truck wasn't in the driveway when the police dropped Keisha at her house. She bristled. He'd promised he'd be here for when Matthew got home from school, which he would be in the next few minutes, unless the boy went to his friend Brendan's house.

Only yesterday she'd been thinking she had to get that man out of her life. Now she'd bound herself to Kirk even more tightly by enlisting his help today. She'd lost all her leverage. How did you kick some-one out when he knew you'd killed a man? Sure, they were in this together, up to a point. Kirk had helped her cover things up, destroyed evidence. But she was betting he could walk into the Milford police station and cut himself a deal if he was willing to roll on her.

So he was more than an accomplice. He was a potential liability. How would he hold up to an interrogation by Detective Wedmore? She seemed to have a pretty good grasp on what had happened at the Garfield house. She was guessing, of course, but Keisha had been too, when she was relating her "vision" to Wendell Garfield, and look how close she'd gotten.

As worried as Keisha was about getting caught, about what would happen to her, there was a greater concern underlying all of this.

What would happen to Matthew?

If the police took her away, if they charged her with murder, if she failed to persuade a jury that she'd acted in self-defense, and was sent to prison, what would happen to her boy?

Here she was, cursing her mother on the one hand, and repeating the pattern she'd set on the other. Raising a child while living on the edges of the law, you had to know that one day it could all blow up in your face. But Keisha'd never considered her crimes as serious as those her mother committed. She didn't hide bodies and steal Social Security checks. She wheedled money out of people, but it was always their choice, ultimately. The people she conned had to know, at some level, that they were being taken advantage of. They knew what was going on, and they didn't mind.

239

Keisha never expected anyone to die.

What about Caroline? she wondered. Her cousin, in San Francisco? Would she take in Matthew, if it came to that?

Caroline, whose mother was Keisha's mother's sister, was a nice, decent woman. She had an honest job as a concierge at the Ritz-Carlton, and a husband named Earl who drove for FedEx. They had three children. Two girls, twelve and fifteen, and a son, seven. Good, hard-working people.

So decent, in fact, that they had little to do with Keisha. She was the family's shame, the one who was raised by the family's previous embarrassment, the one who made her living in a sketchy way, the one who got knocked up by a soldier who'd rather do another tour in Afghanistan than be a father.

But no matter how much Caroline might look down her nose at her cousin, she never took it out on Matthew. Even though she didn't see her second cousin often, she never forgot to phone him on his birthday, or send him a small present at Christmas. This past year, she even mailed him some chocolate eggs at Easter.

Matthew'd be better off with Caroline and Earl, Keisha thought, even if I don't get arrested.

No, no, that wasn't true. For all her faults, Keisha believed she was a good mother. She loved her son more than anything in the world, and he loved her. As long as it was possible for them to be together, they would be.

Should she call her cousin? Keisha contemplated

phoning Caroline, telling her something had come up, she might have to send Matthew out there for a few days. Once he was there, if the police did pick her up, Caroline would hold onto him. She'd do the right thing. She was that kind of person.

These thoughts ran through Keisha's mind as she unlocked the front door of her rented house and walked into the living room. Saw Kirk's unfinished beer and half-eaten Twinkie on the coffee table.

She looked at the clock. Any moment now, Matthew would be home.

Outside, she heard a car door slam. Seconds later, the front door opened and Kirk's eyes landed on her.

"Shit, I raced back here for the kid, but you're already here. You couldn't have called me?"

"I just got dropped off a second ago," Keisha said. "Did you do it? Did you get the bag?"

He smiled triumphantly. "I got the bag."

If there were half a dozen weights on her shoulders, she felt one of them float away. "Oh thank God. It was still there? It hadn't been opened?"

"Still there, not opened," he said. "You think I don't know how to get things done?"

"Okay, that's good. Thank you."

"You get the five grand?"

She nodded tiredly. "I got it."

He slapped his hands together. "Did she get cash, like I told her?"

"She got cash."

"Let's have a look."

241

She pointed to her purse, which she'd dropped onto the couch. He dug into it, found the envelope, and peered inside. He riffled his finger across the tops of the bills.

"Sweet," he said. "Have you counted it?"

"Gail wouldn't cheat me."

"We should go out for dinner tonight and celebrate," Kirk said.

"I don't feel like celebrating."

"Come on. Live a little."

Keisha glared at him. "What's wrong with you?"

"Huh?"

"All the stuff that's gone down today—I nearly died! A man is *dead*. This police woman, Wedmore, is sniffing around me, and I think she knows what happened. And you want to go out and celebrate?"

He had the money out of the envelope and had turned the bills into a thick fan. "You have to live in the moment, babe. And at this moment, we're loaded."

"I almost gave it back," she said quietly.

"You what?"

"I almost gave it back. I'm not taking advantage of people like this any more. You don't think today was some kind of message? Huh? You don't think maybe somebody's trying to tell me something?"

He sneered. "Oh, that's bullshit. Sometimes shit just happens. Then, the next day, different shit happens."

She shook her head and walked into the kitchen.

He followed her in, saying, "Where you wanna go? Come on. The l'il fucker likes Chinese. We'll go someplace he likes."

"His name is Matthew."

"Come on, you know I'm just goofin' around."

She leaned against the counter and sighed. "What did you end up doing with it?" she asked.

"With what?"

"The bag. Where'd you finally dump it?"

"Oh, it's still in the truck," he said offhandedly. "I was planning to get rid of it soon as the kid showed up. Go to the mall, get a snack, drop it off back of the place."

Keisha wondered if she should just turn herself in. It'd be faster. "You're not serious."

"Yeah, I raced back 'cause you wanted someone to be here for the kid. Figured you wouldn't be home in time. I'll get rid of it, don't worry."

"So that bag, it's here, sitting in the driveway?"

"Don't worry. It's all under control. Where is the kid, anyway?"

"I don't know," Keisha said. She left the kitchen and went to the front door to watch for Matthew, saw Kirk's truck parked by her car.

She couldn't see the bag in the back of it.

"Kirk!" she shouted. "I don't see any bag!"

"It's there," he said wearily. "It's just tucked up under the rear window, is all."

She was going to go out and see for herself, but stopped when a dark vehicle stopped at the end of the driveway. An unmarked police car. Rona Wedmore got out, looked at the house, saw Keisha standing in the doorway, and smiled.

"Perfect," Keisha said.

TWENTY-NINE

As Detective Wedmore walked past Kirk's truck, she glanced into the cargo bed, empty save for the green garbage bag with the red tie at the top. Keisha opened the door wide as Wedmore mounted the three steps.

"Detective," she said.

"Ms Ceylon," Wedmore said, nodding. "Mind if I come in?"

Keisha admitted her into the house. Wedmore saw Kirk standing there and said, "Hi, how are you? I'm Detective Wedmore with the Milford police."

Kirk's right hand was busy stuffing the five thousand in cash into the back of his pants, so he awkwardly extended his left. Wedmore accepted it as though she always shook hands that way.

"Hey," he said with false cheerfulness. "I'm Kirk. Nice to meet you." He flashed a smile.

"What'd you do to your face there?"

He touched his scratched cheek. "Nothin'," he said.

"I had an interesting chat with Mrs. Beaudry," Rona Wedmore said to Keisha. "She brought up something I wanted to bounce off you."

"Sure," Keisha said. "Did you want to talk privately?"

"No, this is fine," the detective said, smiling again at Kirk, who still had one hand rubbing the lump of cash in the back of his jeans. "This all comes back to the card."

"My business card," Keisha said.

"That's right. She says . . ." Wedmore stopped herself and looked at Kirk. "I'm sorry, I'm probably being very rude here. Has Ms Ceylon told you about what's happened today?"

"Uh, a little," he said hesitantly. "Some dude got killed or something."

"That's right. Wendell Garfield."

"That's the guy was on TV asking for help to find his wife. Yeah, I know who you mean."

"When we found Mr. Garfield, he had Ms Ceylon's business card in his shirt pocket."

Kirk's eyes went wide. "Wow, well, that's something. Isn't that something, Keisha?"

Shut up, she thought. She should have said it out loud.

Kirk said, "So maybe he was thinking of hiring Keisha to find out what happened to his wife. She does that, you know. She's got this gift. She can see shit." He smiled at her and put a hand on her shoulder. "And she likes to help people."

Shut up shut up shut up.

Wedmore turned her attention back to Keisha. "You had a theory about how Mr. Garfield got your card. A theory that didn't include you handing it to him yourself."

Keisha said, "I don't know how he got my card,

but yes, I do think maybe he could have gotten it from his sister, Gail. Since she's already been coming to see me for some time for consultations."

"Right, that's what you said. So I asked Mrs. Beaudry about that. Whether she had given her brother your card."

Keisha waited.

"And she said it was possible. She didn't actually remember doing it, but she said she could have given it to him, or to Mrs. Garfield."

"Well, there you are," Keisha said, not feeling as relieved as she'd have liked.

"So I asked her how many of your business cards she still has. And she said, so far as she knows, none. Which would seem to mean that the only card she might ever have gotten from you ended up with Mr. Garfield."

"Like she told you, she thinks it was possible."

"Yes. I asked her, if she only ever had the one card from you, when did you actually give it to her."

"Well," Keisha said, "if you're asking me, I have no idea. I hand out cards all the time. I could have had some on the table there and she took one on her way out."

Wedmore nodded, looking at the coffee table decorated with beer and half a Twinkie. "I can see how that might happen. But the thing is, she was able to tell me when it happened. When she got the card. She says you told her earlier today."

"I did?"

"She says you brought it up. She told me that

during a session some time ago—something to do with Amelia Earhart, I think she said?"

"Gail believes she channels the spirits of some notable people throughout history."

"Nuttier than a fruitcake," Kirk said, grinning. "I mean, I'm just sayin'."

Keisha shot him a look, then told Wedmore, "I take all of my clients' beliefs very seriously, Detective, even if Kirk doesn't. I don't mock them."

"No, of course not. Anyway, Mrs. Beaudry was saying that while she was—do you say *channeling*?"

"Yes."

"While she was channeling Amelia Earhart, she says that she asked you for one of your cards because she believed it could help someone. She says you reminded her of that this morning."

"I think—yes, I do believe I mentioned that earlier today."

"But Mrs. Beaudry doesn't actually remember asking for it."

"Often she does not remember discussions she has with me when she's channeling another person."

Wedmore nodded slowly and smiled. "So it was as Amelia Earhart that she asked for this card?"

Keisha sighed. "It's not quite like that. I mean, Gail is still always *Gail*, even when she's channeling someone else. So I believe it was Gail asking for that card. But she may not recall the incident clearly because of the confluence of personalities at the time."

"Uh huh," Wedmore said. "But don't you find it interesting?"

"It's all very interesting. Helping people connect with past lives is fascinating work, Detective."

"No, not that, though I grant you, that is pretty interesting. No, what I find interesting, fascinating, in fact, is that you brought this up *today*. That you happened to remind Mrs. Beaudry about this incident, about giving her a card. And this was before I spoke to you and told you we'd found your card on Mr. Garfield's body. Don't you find that curious?"

There was a noise at the door behind them. They all turned and saw Matthew, backpack slung over his shoulder, coming into the house. He stopped short when he saw the three people—one of whom he'd never seen before—standing there.

"Hey, sweetheart," Keisha said, grateful for the interruption. She moved around Wedmore, greeted her son with a hug and helped him slide the backpack off his shoulders.

"Hey . . . buddy," Kirk said. Matthew didn't look at him as she pulled off his winter coat.

"Who are you?" Matthew asked the detective.

"I'm Rona Wedmore," she said, and Keisha was grateful that she had not identified herself as a police officer. But the feeling was short-lived.

"Are you a cop?" he asked. "That's a cop car out front, isn't it? I can tell because it's got those little hubcaps and the big antenna on the back."

"Yes," she said. "I'm a cop."

"Cool," he said. "How fast can your car go?"

"I've never driven it flat out, but it can go pretty good."

"You ever chased anybody with it?"

"Not that car. But back when I was in uniform, in a regular police car, I chased a couple of people."

"I'd like to do that," Matthew said.

"You have to be really careful, though," Wedmore said. "If the chase starts getting too dangerous, innocent people can get hurt."

Keisha said, "Sweetheart, why don't you go to your room while we finish up talking with the detective."

"You have to help me with my math," he said.

"We can do that later, okay?"

"Okay," he said, and walked away.

"Nice boy," Wedmore said.

Keisha felt a lump in her throat. "Yes."

"Lots of questions about the car, but he wasn't the slightest bit interested in why I might be here."

"He likes cars," Kirk said. "Gonna grow up to be a real car nut, I bet. Kind of like me. You see those wheels over there? They're for my truck."

Wedmore persisted with Keisha. "So, Ms Ceylon, you didn't answer my question."

"I'm sorry, I kind of lost track there." Except she hadn't.

"Don't you think it's curious you'd go to all the trouble of reminding Mrs. Beaudry about the time she asked you for your business card, just before I was going to question you about why Mr. Garfield had one on him?"

Keisha said nothing. Kirk filled the silence. "Like I said before, the woman's a total Froot Loop. I mean, no disrespect intended, and Keisha, she does her best with these nutcases, but come on, you really going to believe anything a woman says who thinks she was Emily Lockhart or whoever you said?"

Wedmore asked him, "So you think Mrs. Beaudry is wrong? That she never did take a card from Ms Ceylon, and never did give it to her brother?"

Kirk made a face that suggested his brain was hurting. "Oh, well, that part, that part sounds about right."

"Mrs. Beaudry strikes me as a—what's the word—suggestible woman," Wedmore said to Keisha. "Would you agree with that?"

"Not . . . necessarily."

"I'm thinking, it wouldn't be that hard to plant an idea in her head. That's what I'm thinking you did with the card. You made her think you gave her a card, when you never gave her one at all."

"I gave her one," Keisha said forcefully. "I'm sure I did."

"A couple of minutes ago, you didn't have any memory of doing that."

"You've reminded me of some things, that's all. There's been a lot going on. I'm still not over being taken into that house, seeing all that blood."

"Sure, I can understand how upsetting it would be to see that again."

Keisha turned on her and said sharply, "I told you, I was never there. You hear me? *Never*. You may think that stupid little card puts me there, but that's bullshit. Complete and total bullshit."

"Yeah," Kirk said.

Now Keisha looked at him, just as angrily. "Don't you have something to do? An errand to run? A delivery?"

He blinked. "Yeah, I do." He nodded at Wedmore. "I should get going."

"I have you blocked in," Wedmore said. "I'll come out with you."

Kirk threw on his coat, pulling it down at the bottom to make sure it covered the bulge of cash. He checked the pocket to make sure he had his keys and said, "So, Keesh, be back in a bit, okay?"

He went out the door, followed by Wedmore. Keisha, worried about anything he might say to the detective, stepped outside, wrapping her arms around herself against the cold.

"You don't have to worry about Keisha," Kirk said. "She's a good person."

"I'm sure," Wedmore said as they approached the truck. "This what you have to deliver?"

She pointed to the bag in the cargo bed.

"Huh?" Kirk said, his hand on the door handle.

"This bag here?"

"More drop off than deliver. Just getting rid of some garbage."

"They don't have pickup on this street?" Wedmore asked.

"Oh sure, but sometimes, you have a lot of stuff, you don't want to wait for garbage day."

"This is hardly a lot of stuff," she said. "It's just one bag."

"Yeah, but we had some fish, and you know, that stuff sits around, it gets pretty ripe by pickup day."

"In the summer, yeah, I could see that," Wedmore said. "But you tuck that in a can, it'll probably freeze these days."

Kirk shrugged, hauled himself up into the driver's seat. "You know, everybody does stuff different."

"So you're really going to make a trip to the dump for this one bag? Isn't that kind of crazy?"

Another shrug. "I just do what the boss tells me."

Keisha, watching this, knew it was all over. She wondered whether Kirk had been born this stupid, or if it was something he'd worked at over the years.

"Where is the dump, anyway?" Wedmore asked.

"Say again?" Kirk, evidently, had just suffered some partial hearing loss.

"I said, where is the dump? In case I ever have a lot of stuff I have to haul out of my place. Where is it?"

"The dump?" Kirk said. "You asking where it is?"

Keisha thought about lawyers. She didn't know any offhand. She didn't want to just pick one at random out of the Yellow Pages. A personal recommendation would be useful.

"That's what I was asking," Wedmore said.

"You just go out Route One, up aways," he said.

"Open the bag," the detective said.

"I'm sorry, what?"

"You heard me. Open the bag."

"It's gonna stink to high heaven," he said. "You sure you want me to do that?"

"Yes."

Wedmore took a couple of steps back, giving Kirk room to slide out of the truck. He stood alongside the cargo bed, reached for the bag, lifted it out by the red ties, and set it on the driveway.

"Mom, can I have something to eat?"

Keisha whirled around, saw Matthew standing there. "Go to your room!" she shouted.

The boy, startled, bolted.

"Open it," Wedmore said.

The red ties were knotted, so Kirk had to poke a finger into the green plastic of the bag and make a tear in it. He glanced back at Keisha, giving her an apologetic grimace before enlarging the opening. Once he'd created a hole about the size of a paper plate, Wedmore asked him to step away.

She leaned over the bag, peered inside, then looked at Kirk. "I don't see any fish in here."

"No?"

"No. I see a lot of pizza scraps, but no fish."

Kirk blinked. "I guess I got mixed up," he said.

THIRTY

The dumb son of a bitch had grabbed the wrong bag.

This had to be a first, Keisha thought. Kirk's stupidity paying off. It would have been better if he'd come back without any bag at all, but if he had to bring one home, better that it be filled with discarded pizza.

Of course, it meant that bag of bloody clothes was still in the Dumpster behind that pizza place. Maybe, Keisha prayed to herself, it would end up getting picked up on trash day without ever being discovered.

The bag wasn't her biggest problem at the moment, anyway. It was that damned card.

If the card was the only thing that could place her at the Garfield house, Keisha believed she could ride it out. Couldn't any lawyer with half a brain come up with a dozen ways it could have ended up in the dead man's shirt pocket?

She tried to stay composed as Wedmore, now wearing rubber gloves, sifted through the bag of garbage. There were pizza scraps, empty pop cans and water bottles, cardboard triangles for takeout slices, napkins.

She could hear Wedmore asking Kirk more questions.

"Where would you get all this?" she asked.

"We had pizza the other night," he said.

"This isn't garbage from one night's pizza," the detective said. "This is like trash from a restaurant."

"No, it's from here," he insisted. "The li'l—the kid, he had a pizza party with some of his friends. They made a hell of a mess. I think they had some fish sticks, too, which is why I mentioned fish, why I wanted to get it out of the house."

Keisha could just guess who Wedmore would want to talk to next: Matthew. She'd want to ask him when his pizza party had been. How many friends had he had over? What were their names?

Just when you thought things were turning a corner.

She went back into the house and rapped lightly on Matthew's bedroom door before she opened it.

He was sitting on his bed, playing with a handheld video game, and made a point of not looking at his mother as she came into the room.

"I'm sorry, honey," Keisha said. "I'm sorry I yelled at you."

"I didn't do *anything*," he said.

"I know that. It's just, things have been a little tense around here today."

"Why's the police lady here?" It had finally occurred to him to ask.

"A man died," Keisha said.

"What man?"

"No one we know, sweetheart. But he had one of my business cards in his pocket, somehow, so the lady was asking me if I knew him."

"What happened to the man? Was he in an accident or was he shot or something?"

Keisha felt more tired now than she had felt all day. "He was . . . stabbed."

"So she's trying to find out who stabbed him?"

Keisha sat on the edge of the bed and rested her hand on her son's knee. "Yes, that's what she's trying to do."

"So there's like a crazy person running around stabbing people?" he asked, but more excited than fearful.

"No, not a crazy person," Keisha said. "It may even be that this man who died was the bad person, and that whoever stabbed him had a reason. Like, to protect herself." She paused, and added, "Or himself."

"Oh, yeah, like, self-defense." Matthew watched his share of crime shows.

"Could be," Keisha said. "Let me ask you something."

Matthew put aside his video game. "What?"

"Winters here are pretty cold and miserable. How would you feel about maybe spending some time in California?"

"You mean, like, in San Francisco? With your cousin?"

"I haven't asked her about it, but yeah, that was kind of what I was thinking."

"When would we go?"

Keisha touched the side of his head gently. "I was thinking it would be a trip just for you. You being ten, and all, you're getting to be a young man. It'd be a chance for you to fly all by yourself."

He shook his head. "I don't know. I don't think I want to go by myself. Except maybe for a weekend or something."

Keisha thought, how about five to ten years?

"I'm not exactly Caroline's favorite cousin in the world, but she loves you, and would be very happy to see you. She'd probably be even happier if I stayed here."

"Why doesn't she like you?" Matthew asked.

Keisha smiled sadly. "I think she likes me okay. She's just disappointed in me. Sometimes I'm a little disappointed in me too."

"I'm not disappointed in you," Matthew said. "But I hate Kirk."

Keisha nodded. "Yeah, I get that. Listen, we can talk about that later, but right now, I need you to scoot. Why don't you go hang out with Brendan?"

"I guess. Why do I have to go?"

"I may have to talk to the police lady again, and I don't think she likes to talk about police business in front of kids."

"Oh."

"And I want you to go out the back way."

"Why?"

"She's out front right now, talking to Kirk, and I don't think she'd want you interrupting them."

"Is Kirk in trouble?" the boy asked hopefully.

"I—I don't think so."

258

Matthew frowned. "I was hoping maybe he was the stabber, that they'd take him away."

"Oh, baby."

"Is he always going to live with us?'

"Matthew, I don't even know what's going to happen an hour from now."

"Do you love him?" Matthew asked.

"Love Kirk?"

He nodded.

"I thought I did, when I first met him, when he was different. But no, not any more. Why?"

"I was worried you loved him more than me."

"What?" she said, wrapping her arms around the boy and squeezing. "How could you even ask such a thing?" She could feel him shrug, trapped in her embrace. "No, come on, I want an answer." She released him, put a finger under his chin and propped his head up so he'd have to look her in the eye. "Why would you say that?"

"Something Kirk told me."

"What'd he say?"

"He said I wasn't supposed to know, so I couldn't talk about it, especially to you."

"Matt, listen to me. You can tell me anything. You know that."

"It's just, when you said I might be going to California, I thought maybe that's where the military school is." The boy looked like he was trying very hard to hold back tears.

"What military school? You're ten years old, for God's sake."

"Kirk said they have one for kids like me, and if I didn't stop, you know, messing up around here, and touching his wheels, and getting in the way, he said you were going to send me away to that school."

"He said *what*?"

"He said if I settled down you'd probably forget about it, so that's why I've been staying in my room a lot so I won't be in the way because I really don't want to go to that school and learn how to fight and kill people and stuff."

"That son of a bitch," she said under her breath, but still not caring if Matthew heard.

"So that's not why you want me to go stay with your cousin?"

"Look at me. If I have to send you out there, it won't be because you did anything wrong, or that you're going to a military academy, and it won't mean I don't love you."

"So there's no military school?"

"There's no military school."

Matthew cracked a smile. "Are you crying, Mom?"

"Maybe a little."

"I think I'm going to, too. But I'm happy."

"Look, just give me a hug, and then get the hell out of here, okay?"

The boy and his mother threw their arms around one another again. Then he grabbed his coat and disappeared out the back door of the house, hopped the fence, and was gone.

★

A knock at the door again.

"I thought you'd left, Detective," Keisha said. She noticed the unmarked car had moved ahead far enough to allow Kirk to leave in his truck. But the bag of pizza trash was still sitting on the driveway.

They'll figure out what pizza place it's all from. They'll go there, search the Dumpster.

"I'd like to speak with your son," Wedmore said.

"Matthew's not here."

Wedmore looked surprised. "I didn't see him come out of the house."

"He went out the back. He's gone to see a friend."

"Which friend?"

"I don't know. He didn't say."

"One of the friends he had over for his pizza party?"

Keisha nodded. "Possibly."

"When was this party?" the detective asked.

"Just in the last few days. Yesterday? No, the day before I think it was. Did Kirk take off?"

"He did. Said he still had some errands to run, other than going to the dump. He must be quite the neat freak, wanting to make a trip to the dump to drop off a single bag of trash from a pizza party."

Keisha said nothing while the detective studied her. Wedmore was thinking something, Keisha could tell. Plotting her next move.

Finally the detective said, "You have a nice day, Ms Ceylon." She let herself out, grabbed the bag of trash as she passed it, dropped it into the trunk of her unmarked car, and drove off.

Keisha closed the door and half stumbled back into her house. She went down the hall, into her son's room, and collapsed on his bed. She pulled his pillow into her face and rolled her body into a ball, comforting herself with the scent of him.

Kirk, that son of a bitch, she thought. Telling her son she was going to send him away. She could only begin to imagine the thoughts that must have been going through Matthew's head. What kind of man would put that fear into a child?

Of all the things he'd done, this was the worst.

She couldn't allow the anger she felt for this man to overtake her. She needed to keep a clear head, to figure out what Wedmore might do next and what, if anything, she could do to protect herself.

Was it possible Rona Wedmore was going to return with a search warrant? Maybe bring along a team of *CSI*-type people, except they wouldn't have fabulous hair and be dressed in the coolest clothes. They'd be in white suits that made them look like spacemen, and they'd very likely have some hi-tech gadget that would reveal blood that was invisible to the naked eye.

Keisha hoped she and Kirk had done a thorough enough job cleaning the house. If they'd got rid of all the blood, she should be in the clear on that—

No, there were other things to get rid of.

The money. She'd kept the cash Garfield had given her. Tucked it behind the toilet paper under the bathroom sink. Was there any blood on it? Wasn't that something she'd meant to check later? Before

Gail showed up, and she was dragged back into that house of horrors?

She swung her legs off the bed, started off in the direction of the bathroom.

The phone rang.

Keisha wanted to ignore it, but thought it might be Matthew. She ran for her bedroom and picked up the extension on an old phone that did not have call display.

"Hello?"

"Keisha, it's Gail."

"Oh. Yes, Gail?"

"That lady detective? She got me all confused."

Keisha closed her eyes tiredly. "Yeah. About my card."

"That's right!"

"She was here a few minutes ago."

"I told her you'd given me one of your cards, and that somewhere along the line I must have passed it on to Wendell, but then she started asking me when this all came up, and I told her you mentioned it to me this morning, and—"

"I know, I know."

"And the other thing I called about," Gail said hesitantly, "was if, since you got back home, was, you know, if . . ."

"If something comes to me," Keisha said, "I'll call you immediately."

"Okay, that's fine. Listen, I have to go. There's family to call, I'm going to have to get in touch with the funeral home and—"

"Goodbye Gail."

Keisha replaced the receiver in its cradle and was about to turn away when the phone rang again, so quickly it made her jump.

She snatched up the receiver before the first ring had finished and said, "Gail, please, I can't talk—"

"Hey," Kirk said. "It's me."

You told my son I was going to get rid of him.

They were the first words that came into her head, but what she said aloud was, "What?"

"I got good news."

She found that hard to believe, but summoned the energy to ask what it was just the same.

"I went back."

"Back where?"

"I got the bag. The *right* bag. I parked next door again, snuck over, opened the bin when there was no one around, and got it. I peeked inside, saw the clothes, made sure, right? I figured, that bitch cop, when she saw the pizza, she might start sniffing around at pizza places all over, you know, and—"

"Tell me you're not bringing it home."

"Jeez, Keesh, I'm not an idiot. I already got rid of it. In a Dumpster out back of a different plaza, blocks away. And *no one* saw me this time. That's good, right?"

"Yeah," she said weakly, afraid to feel encouraged. "That's good."

It was, she conceded to herself, welcome news. If the police didn't find the clothes, and if they didn't turn up any blood in the house or the car, she might—just might—get through this.

So long as they didn't show up at the door in the next five seconds to search the house.

"So, whaddya say *now* about a little celebration tonight? You me and the l'il fucker?"

The brief sense of relief she'd felt was displaced by hatred and contempt.

"We'll see," she said.

"Be home in a bit." He ended the call.

"Finally," she said, and strode out of her bedroom. She was swinging open the door of the cabinet below the bathroom sink when she was interrupted again.

This time, a knock at the door.

"No," she said. "Please no."

It seemed too soon for Wedmore to have returned with a warrant and a forensics team, but Keisha imagined the police could move quickly when they wanted to.

She swung open the door, expecting the worst.

And in a way, that was what she got. But it was not Rona Wedmore standing there on the front step, grinning at her.

It was Justin.

Parked at the curb was his stepfather's Range Rover, but there was so sign of Dwayne Taggart.

"Hey," Justin said. "I figured out another way to make a little more money, and I wanted to tell you about it."

THIRTY-ONE

"Not a good time, Justin," Keisha said, blocking the door. The kid had always given her the creeps, but there was something about the grin on his face now that was particularly unsettling.

"Oh, I really think you're going to want to hear this," he said, his hands shoved into the front pockets of his jeans, his shoulders hunched, trying to fight off the cold in nothing more than a light sports jacket and sneakers. "Let me come in and I'll tell you about it."

"No," she said, barring the door.

"Seriously? You don't even know what I've got to say."

"Justin, go away."

"You look really stressed out, Keisha. Everything okay?" There was nothing in his expression that suggested empathy. He looked—was this possible?—mischievous.

"I haven't had a very good day," she said.

"I'll just bet you haven't."

She was starting to close the door on him when he said that, and she stopped. "What's that supposed to mean?"

"I'm just saying, I bet you've had a pretty stressful day."

She tried to read him, figure out what his game was. "You got something you want to say?"

"It's kind of cold out here," he said, on the verge of shivering. Reluctantly, she opened the door and allowed him in. He took his hands out of his pockets and rubbed them together. "I shoulda worn something warmer. But I really hate big coats and boots and all that. Makes you feel like you're smothering."

"Why are you here?" Keisha said, closing the door.

"Like I said, I got this idea to make more money." He offered an apologetic smile. "Actually, it's an idea for *me* to make more money. But even so, I think you're going to want to hear it."

She waited.

"So, you gonna invite me into the living room or anything?"

"No."

He looked hurt, then made a quick recovery. "Okay, so, this morning, when I dropped by, as I was leaving, you were watching the news about the guy whose wife went missing on Thursday. There was that press conference, with his daughter, getting all weepy and stuff? You remember?"

She hesitated. "Yes."

That grin. "I knew you would. And I was thinking, that's your thing. Like with the Archers. I could tell your interest was, what's the word, piqued. And you know, so was mine. I thought it would be cool to see how you work your magic."

No.

"Remember I said we should work together? How I would like to job-shadow you, like we used to do in high school? And you basically said to piss off?" He shook his head. "That never really works with me. I'm not real good at following instructions. It's what all my teachers said, even Mr. Archer."

"What did you do, Justin?"

"Okay, so, Dwayne—still a big fan of yours, by the way, for finding me, and even my mom can't get her head around how you did it—drove me over here this morning, right, and on the way back home I said, hey Dwayne, my man, would it be okay if I borrowed the car for a while? Just to drive around and clear my head? Because for the last week, he and my mom have been all over me, thinking I'm gonna run away again or try to kill myself, right?" He leaned his head toward hers, like there were others in the room and he wanted to tell her a secret. "Between you and me, I really do wonder whether our scheme was such a good idea. I mean, yeah, I got the money we split and they're all worried sick about me and all, but Christ almighty, they're watching me like a hawk, you know? I look in the fridge and sigh because we're out of ice cream and they think I'm going to slit my wrists." He laughed.

"Anyway, so I say to Dwayne, I'm feeling really good and would you trust me to borrow the Rover for a spin or something. Said it would lift my spirits, help me clear my head. And he tosses me the keys. So then I look up this Garfield guy's address and plug it into the ol' GPS, and by the time I drive by, your car's already out front. Like, perfect timing."

Keisha felt as though she needed to sit down, but kept standing.

"So I parked down a side street and hoofed it back and I was actually thinking maybe I'd knock on the door and introduce myself as your assistant, you know? But I thought first I should see how it was going, and I got this great spot in the garden, by the living room on the side of the house, where the blinds hadn't been closed, where I could see you do your thing. I couldn't hear much, but I was able to get the gist of it, watching you make your pitch, then Garfield looking all, like, you gotta be kiddin' me. So I'm watching for a while, and pretty soon Garfield brings down a bathrobe or whatever it was and you start running your fingers all over it."

He shook his head in wonderment. "I gotta ask, what the hell made him snap?"

Keisha, speechless, didn't know which fact left her more stunned. That Justin had seen the whole thing, or that he'd chosen to do nothing when he saw it.

"I mean, I was totally blown away. Even if he thought you were there to scam him, why would he try to kill you, right? Why not just kick you out on your ass, like the Archers did, or call the cops?" He nodded his head encouragingly, trying to provoke a response. "What was going on?"

Keisha, her voice no more than a whisper, said, "I got . . . lucky. My vision was too close to the truth.

His daughter killed Mrs. Garfield and he helped her cover it up."

Justin's mouth opened. The shock was genuine. "No shit? Whoa, that's crazy. That must have blown your fucking mind."

Quietly. "Yeah."

"So he's strangling you, and you grab the—what was it, one of those needles for stitching things?"

"Yes."

"And you get him right in the eye. Backhand! That was awesome! Watching him stagger around with that thing coming out of his head, that was fucking unreal. I thought you had the upper hand, but then, when he still went after you, I thought, Jesus, even with a stick in his brain the bastard just won't stop. Like in a movie, you know? I didn't think you were going to make it, but I was pullin' for ya, I really was."

"He nearly killed me," Keisha said, touching her hand to her neck. "And you watched."

Justin shrugged. "Couldn't very well go busting in and have people think I was some sort of peeping Tom pervert. Anyway, you handled yourself just fine. After you took off, so did I." He rubbed his hands together again. "So, you want to hear my idea?"

"I'm betting I can guess."

"I want your half."

"What?"

"The money Dwayne gave you for finding me. I know we agreed to split it, but now I want it all. And . . ." He rubbed his chin. "Another two grand on top of that ought to do it. Let's call it forty-five hundred. You give me that, and I don't tell the cops what I saw."

"If you tell the cops what you saw, then you're saying you were there."

Justin waved his index finger at her. "Good point. But there's nothing to say I can't make an anonymous call, is there? Maybe confirm a few things for the cops. Get them looking in the right direction."

"You'd do that," Keisha said.

Justin laughed. "Hey, I'm doing you a favor here. You don't see me going to the cops first. I've come here with an opportunity for you. And you know what else I was thinking? I was thinking, you and me, we should work together in the future. We make a good team."

"I don't know that I can get you that kind of money," Keisha said. There was the five grand from Gail Beaudry, but right now it was in Kirk's back pocket. How likely was he to surrender it? Hesitantly, she said, "I don't know if Kirk will give it to me."

"Kirk? That's your boyfriend?"

She hesitated again. "Yes."

"You saying he won't give it to you? To keep you from getting arrested?"

"He'll take some convincing."

Justin asked, "Does he know what went down today?" Keisha nodded. "Then you need to talk to him. Convince him."

"Maybe you should ask him yourself. I'm expecting him back in a little while."

Justin nodded confidently. "Okay, good, I'll talk to him. I can wait. I'm guessing he's not gonna want his sweetie to get into any trouble."

"Yeah," Keisha said flatly. "He's always thinking of me first."

THIRTY-TWO

Justin was getting antsy standing by the front door, so he went uninvited into the living room and plopped down onto the couch. He cast his eye over the half-full beer bottle and the Twinkie remnants. "You got anything to drink?"

"No," Keisha said.

"Some host," he muttered under his breath. "So tell me, what'd you do after you left Garfield's house? You must have been a mess. You go through a car wash with all the windows open?"

She didn't answer him. She was at the window, watching for Kirk.

"Fine, ignore me," Justin said. "So this boyfriend of yours, what's he do? Does he predict the future, or track down aliens, or some other shit like that?"

"He works construction," Keisha said. "But not for a while. He hurt his foot. But he's walking okay now."

"That's nice," Justin said. "I look forward to doing business with him."

Keisha heard a familiar rumbling, then saw Kirk's truck turn into the driveway. The truck bed, as far as she could see, really was empty. Kirk got out and came strutting up the walk like a man who was not only proud of himself, but expecting to get laid.

He came into the house and said, "Hey. Babe!"

"In here," Keisha said.

He took a couple of steps into the house and scanned his eyes across the living room. Justin stood and extended a hand.

"Hey, how ya doin'," he said. Kirk shook his hand, his face a puzzle. "Don't think we've ever actually been introduced. I'm Justin. Last time I was here, you were still snoozing." He grinned. "Had to keep my voice down. Keisha here didn't want to disturb the beast."

Kirk didn't know what was going on. He'd never met Justin, although Keisha had told him about the scam she'd run with him. Only thing was, she'd told him her share was a thousand, not twenty-five hundred.

"Justin and I did that job together," Keisha reminded him. "His parents hired me to find him? We set it up ahead?"

"Oh yeah, right," Kirk said. "Nice."

"Yeah," Justin said, smiling. "My idea, totally. I was just telling Keisha here, we should do some more work together."

Kirk shrugged, like maybe that was a good idea. "That why you're here now? You cooking up something?"

"No, this is about something else," Keisha said.

"Keisha tells me you're all up to speed on what happened today," Justin said.

Kirk eyed him warily. Even he wasn't dumb

enough to admit to anything until he knew what it was Justin knew.

"Possibly," he said slowly.

Justin understood his caution. "The Garfield house. I know all about it."

Kirk glared at Keisha. "What the hell were you thinking?"

"I didn't tell him," Keisha said. "He was *there*. Looking through the window. Spying."

"Well," Justin said, "I think *spying* is a tad judgmental. Especially considering you went there to rip him off. And really, it wasn't spying. I was just hoping to broaden my horizons, see how Keisha did her thing. Who knew she'd moved from bullshit predictions to eye surgery?"

"How would he even know to be there?" Kirk asked.

Keisha quickly explained that Justin had been by the house in the morning, suspected she might go see Wendell Garfield, and found her at the man's house.

"Yeah," Justin said proudly. "And my mom says I lack initiative."

But even with all this explanation, Kirk was still confused. "So what are you doing here, if you're not planning something new?"

"He's here to blackmail me," Keisha said.

"What?"

"He wants money to keep quiet about what he's seen."

Kirk, reflexively, reached around and touched the bulge under the back of his winter coat.

"How much?" he asked.

"Forty-five hundred," Justin offered cheerily. "That's Keisha's share out of the scam we pulled on my parents, plus another two grand."

Keisha thought, *Nuts*. She could see Kirk doing the math in his head. He looked like a caveman trying to figure out how to take pictures with a smartphone. He said to her, "You told me you only got a thousand out of that job."

Keisha shrugged. "You got me."

Kirk would deal with her later. To Justin, he said, "So you're asking for nearly five grand or you tell the cops Keisha killed Garfield."

"Good," Justin said, like Kirk was five. "You deserve a sticker."

Kirk said, "And you figure we're just going to give it to you."

"Don't you think it would be kind of dumb not to? I make an anonymous call to the cops and they'll be over here. And if you've been helping her cover up what she did, that makes you an accomplice, so it's as much in your interest to keep this all under wraps as it is hers." He waited for some kind of response. "Hello?"

"Yeah, yeah, I'm hearing you," Kirk said, stepping further into the living room, crowding Justin and forcing him to take a couple of steps back. "Well, you're kind of in luck, as it turns out, because I've got the money on me."

Not exactly what Keisha was expecting. She looked at him, dumbfounded.

"No shit?" Justin said, like a junkie seconds away from a fix. "You're kidding, right? No one carries that kind of money on them. I'd have given you a couple of days to get it together."

"No, no, I got it," Kirk said, and reached behind him for the wad of cash Gail had given Keisha.

"Fuck me," Justin said, not believing it as Kirk fanned out the bills in his two hands.

"I'm gonna keep five hundred back, because there's five grand here," Kirk said.

"Shit, you rob a bank or something?" The kid couldn't take his eyes off the money.

Kirk took the five hundred and shoved it into the front pocket of his jeans. He extended the rest of the money to Justin, and just as the young man was about to take it, Kirk let the money fall to the floor. It fluttered like giant confetti.

"Oh shit, sorry, thought you had it there," Kirk said.

"Hey, no problem," Justin said, and dropped to his knees to collect the scattered bills.

Kirk brought up his knee and caught Justin on the nose.

"Fuck!" he screamed, stumbling back, throwing both hands over his face, blood trickling out between his fingers. "What the hell?"

He turned his face away defensively and flailed blindly at Kirk with his bloodied hands like a bullied schoolboy. Kirk deflected Justin's feeble blow with one sweep of his arm, then glanced down at the bloodstains that flecked his shirt. "Shit," he said, and slammed Justin into the wall to the right of the shelves displaying his new wheels.

"You think you can come in here and pull this kind of shit?" Kirk said. "You think I'm just gonna hand you that money?"

"Don't hurt me!" Justin screamed. "I think you broke my nose! Jesus!"

"I'm gonna break every bone in your body if you think you're going to leave here with one fucking cent."

"I'll tell!" he shouted. "The cops'll be all over her!"

Kirk closed the distance between them and put his hands around the young man's neck, just the way he'd done with Keisha earlier in the day.

Justin coughed. "Can't . . ."

It was Justin's turn to use his knee. He brought it up fast and hard, catching Kirk in the testicles.

"Shit!"

Kirk let go of Justin's neck and closed in on himself, hands over his crotch, the pain radiating through him. He stepped back and to the left.

Justin reached out with his right hand, slipped it between the wall and the shelf, and, putting everything he had into it, pushed forward. The shelf was not secured to the wall, and with two wheels on the top, two in the center, and none on the bottom, it was unsteady to begin with.

It teetered, in slow motion at first, then with a gathering momentum.

The two wheels on top pitched off first. One

280

caught Kirk on the shoulder, knocking him to the floor. A fraction of a second later, the other wheel landed on his upper body and flipped over once, covering his face, the edge of the rim pressing against his neck.

As the unit continued its plunge, the two wheels on the middle shelf fell off. One landed on Kirk's knee, while the other hit the carpet.

"Yeah!" Justin said. "Take that, asshole!"

He spun around, giddy, grinned at Keisha, just in time to see the beer bottle coming at his head.

As soon as she hit him, she dropped the bottle. She felt the pain of the impact—the bottle hit him solidly on the forehead—shoot right up her arm. The bottle didn't break, not even when it hit the floor, but it did the trick. Justin staggered backwards and collapsed, hitting the wall next to where the shelf had been and sliding on his back to the floor.

Keisha stood there, her labored breathing the only sound in the room.

She surveyed the wreckage. The overturned shelf, the scattered wheels, Kirk trapped beneath the wreckage. Justin unconscious.

At least, she thought he was unconscious.

"Jesus," she said.

She knelt down, put her hand on Justin's chest. He was out cold, but alive. She could feel him breathing under her palm.

Kirk was alive, too. He made a weak coughing sound.

"Babe," he said. "I can't . . . I can't move."

He made a gagging sound. Keisha moved toward him, put one leg over one of the shelving unit's vertical posts, straddling it so she could get a look at Kirk. She could see one eye behind the wheel, saw how the rim was pressing against Kirk's windpipe. The shelf had landed on top of the wheel, pinning it into position.

Keisha would have to move the shelf before she could get the wheel off him.

"Hey," Kirk said. "Get this . . . get this off me." He was trying to use his hands to move the rim, but one was caught behind his back, and he couldn't get any leverage with the free one.

Keisha thought.

Surveyed the situation.

Thought about Matthew.

Maybe there was still a way out of this. A way for her to stay out of trouble, stay with her boy.

"Hey!" Kirk said. "You . . . fucking deaf? I need . . . help here." He coughed.

There was a lot to figure out in a short time. She'd have to have it done before Justin woke up.

But what she had here was an opportunity.

"Hey," Keisha said, looking down at Kirk through the openings between the mag wheel spokes.

"Can't . . . breathe," he said.

"Looks bad," she said. "Must hurt like a son of a bitch."

"The fuck . . . you doing? Move . . . the shelf." He was sounding wheezy.

"I think I've got a way out, Kirk," she said. "It

might not work, but then again, it might. Got to take the chance."

"What . . . you . . ."

"But it's not going to work with you. Once Wedmore gets you in a room and starts putting questions to you, well, I don't think you're going to be able to outsmart her, you know what I'm saying?"

". . . bitch . . ."

"You're my weak link, Kirk. Sorry. You were an okay guy, you know? When we met? I really fell for you. You seemed so sweet." There was that lump in her throat again. "But you conned me. You got inside me"—and she put her hand between her breasts— "before I realized what a useless piece of shit you are."

He didn't say anything. He was watching her with that one eye.

"But even a couple of hours ago, I might not have been capable of this. I might have helped you out here. But what you told Matthew? That I was going to send him away to military school?" She shook her head, and a teardrop fell from her cheek, slipped between the spokes and landed on Kirk's forehead. "That was the last straw."

"Babe . . ."

She put her weight on the shelf, which in turn forced the wheel down harder on Kirk's neck. She managed to lift one foot from the floor, perch it on the edge of the middle shelf, then the other foot.

Kirk made some very bad sounds. Sounds that Keisha would be hearing for the rest of her life.

She sat there a couple of minutes until she was

sure, glancing every few seconds at Justin to make sure he hadn't regained consciousness.

Once she was certain Kirk was dead, she went into action.

She moved with deliberate speed, thinking through everything carefully.

Rehearsed the story in her head.

Got all the props in place.

Then she found in her jacket pocket the card that Rona Wedmore had given her at the Garfield house. Went to the phone in the bedroom and entered the number.

Wedmore picked up on the third ring.

"Hello?"

"It's Keisha Ceylon. I've got a confession to make."

THIRTY-THREE

Justin: Shit, it's about time. I've been sitting in here for hours. This room—is this one of those interrogation rooms?—this room is freezing. They took my jacket, and they even took my shoes. Why the hell did they take my shoes?

Wedmore: Sorry about that, Justin. Let me see if I can turn the heat up in here. I don't even know if this thermostat is working. How are you feeling?

Justin: My head feels like it's going to blow up. Thanks for asking. That bitch hit me right in the head with a beer bottle. She's crazy. Nearly as crazy as her boyfriend. Both of them are nutcases.

Wedmore: The doctor says you might have a mild concussion. But the good news is, your nose isn't broken.

Justin: Sure feels like it. I want to go home. Is my mom here?

Wedmore: I'm not sure. Listen, they explain to you about the lawyer and everything?

Justin: Oh yeah, but I'm cool. You're gonna want to hear what I have to say about Keisha and that guy.

Wedmore: That's good, because I have a few questions for you before you go.

Justin: Have you charged that asshole with trying to kill me?

Wedmore: You talking about Kirk?

Justin: Yeah.

Wedmore: Kirk Nicholson's dead, Justin.

Justin: Dead?

Wedmore: Yup.

Justin: Well, shit. That must have happened when the shelf fell on him? And those wheels fell off? Is that what happened?

Wedmore: Why did you go to Keisha Ceylon's house?

Justin: I, uh, I wanted to thank her again for finding me before I did anything to hurt myself. I got depressed a couple of weeks back, was in a pretty dark place, and my parents hired her to use her, you know, senses, to find me.

Wedmore: I know that's not true, Justin. Why did you really go there?

Justin: Huh? No, that's true.

Wedmore: So you came by just to say thanks, and that led to a big fight? That ended up with one man dead?

Justin: It's all kind of a blur.

Wedmore: You sure you didn't come by to boast?

Justin: Boast?

Wedmore: That you'd beaten Keisha at her own game?

Justin: I don't—what?

Wedmore: Keisha decided to come clean.

Justin: Come clean? What? She confessed?

Wedmore: She told us a few things.

Justin: She told you she killed that Garfield guy?

Wedmore: No, she didn't confess to that, Justin.

Justin: Well what the hell else would she confess to? She killed that guy.

Wedmore: We can get back to that in a moment. No, what Keisha confessed to was the trick you played on your mother and stepfather.

Justin: I don't . . . I don't know what you mean.

Wedmore: Keisha says you approached her with an idea about how you could take them for five thousand dollars.

Justin: She *told* you about that?

Wedmore: Where'd you get the idea?

Justin: I don't know what you're talking about. Like I said, I was depressed, I ran away from home for a while. My parents hired that woman to find me. She had this vision of me in an empty office my mom used to rent out to some plastic surgery place.

Wedmore: Where'd you go to school, Justin?

Justin: School?

Wedmore: Did you ever have a teacher named Terry Archer?

Justin: Mr. Archer? Yeah, I had an English teacher named Mr. Archer.

Wedmore: I just got off the phone with him. He remembers you.

Justin: He does?

Wedmore: Yeah. He says he remembers a class where he got talking about that horrible thing that happened to him and his wife. He says you were in that class, that you had lots of questions.

Justin: I remember something about that. His wife's family disappeared or something.

Wedmore: Very good. You remember. And I guess you remember the part where Mr. Archer told his students about a psychic who said she'd tell them what happened to the family for a thousand dollars?

Justin: I didn't always pay attention in school.

Wedmore: Mr. Archer says you actually asked him, after class, for the name of the psychic.

Justin: I suppose that's possible, but I don't remember.

Wedmore: Didn't you tell your stepfather, Mr. Taggart, about her? I understand your father has an interest in that sort of thing.

Justin: I don't know where you're going with this.

Wedmore: When Keisha Ceylon led your parents to you, it wasn't the first time you'd met her, was it?

Justin: Uh . . .

Wedmore: You knew what she did, the kind of scams she ran, and you came up with an idea to get five thousand dollars from your parents. After some persuading, Ms Ceylon went along with it.

Justin: Look, my mom, my stepdad, they've got tons of money, and anything I might have done where they're concerned, that's our business. It's not like the public got ripped off or anything. Keisha—she really told you about all this?

Wedmore: She said you're an admirer of her work. A fan. That she inspired you. That after you ran this game on your parents, you wanted to do more work with her, but she said no. Does that sound about right?

288

Justin: I wouldn't say that.

Wedmore: What part do I have wrong? Straighten me out here.

Justin: I don't know. I just . . . none of that rings a bell.

Wedmore: No? You saying you didn't go to Mr. Garfield's house and offer to provide the same kind of service Keisha did?

Justin: Shit, no. Don't you see what she's doing? She's confessed to this other thing, with my mom and her husband and me, because she figures— because it'll make her look almost honest. You know? She's willing to admit all that, so you'll believe her when she says she didn't do the really big thing, killing that guy.

Wedmore: You didn't drop by her house and tell her you were the new fake psychic in town? That you got a thousand bucks out of Mr. Garfield before she did? And that made her boyfriend so angry, you cutting in on his girlfriend's territory, that he attacked you? That there was a fight, and you knocked that bookshelf over on him?

Justin: Okay, that's totally not—there was a fight, yeah, but not the way you're laying it out.

Wedmore: You didn't threaten her son if she gave you a hard time about it?

Justin: Threaten her—what?

Wedmore: Is that why there's a picture of him on your phone? That you emailed to her. So she'd know you were watching him, and not turn you in?

Justin: This is totally—the kid asked me to take his picture.

Wedmore: I've got a couple of things in this box here I want to show you. Hang on . . . here we go. You ever seen this money before, Justin?

Justin: Where's that from?

Wedmore: I'm asking, have you ever seen it.

Justin: It's money. Money's money. It all looks the same.

Wedmore: You notice the blood on the edge of some of the bills there?

Justin: Uh, yeah, I can see that. So?

Wedmore: We've saved out a couple of the bills and are having them tested, but we think that's going to turn out to be Wendell Garfield's blood.

Justin: Oh.

Wedmore: You know where we found this money, Justin?

Justin: I don't know. If it's Garfield's blood, I guess you found that money on Keisha.

Wedmore: We found this money in your jacket, Justin.

Justin: Huh?

Wedmore: How do you think this money got into your jacket?

Justin: Seriously? She put it there. She must have. When I was out cold.

Wedmore: Yeah, I suppose that could have happened. I see your point. You were out for about ten minutes, the doctor said.

Justin: Yeah, well. There you go.

Wedmore: Do me a favor, Justin?

Justin: What?

Wedmore: Would you write your name on this piece of paper here?

Justin: What for?

Wedmore: Just humor me.

Justin: You going to tape it onto the end of some fake confession?

Wedmore: No, we're not going to do that. Let me see if this pen has any ink . . . yeah, this one'll do. Here you go.

Justin: You just want me to write my name?

Wedmore: First and last.

Justin: I don't get this.

Wedmore: Justin . . .

Justin: Fine, fuck it. There you go. Three times.

Wedmore: Thank you. Is that the way you usually sign your name?

Justin: Yeah.

Wedmore: Hmm.

Justin: What?

Wedmore: Just asking. I have something else here I'd like to show you.

Justin: What?

Wedmore: I've got it in another evidence bag, although we found it tucked in with the cash. Okay, here it is. You recognize this, Justin?

Justin: What the . . . it's a check.

Wedmore: That's right. You see whose account this check is drawn on?

Justin: Garfield. Wendell Garfield.

Wedmore: For five hundred and eighty dollars.

Justin: Yeah.

Wedmore: And you see there's also some blood on the edge of the check. We'll have to do a test to see whose blood it is, but like with the money, we have a pretty good idea.

Justin: Okay.

Wedmore: And I guess you've noticed the other interesting thing. The most interesting thing of all.

Justin: That doesn't make any sense to me.

Wedmore: You see who the check is made out to, don't you, Justin?

Justin: I don't know. I can barely read it.

Wedmore: Oh, come on now. What's it say?

Justin: It sort of looks like my name.

Wedmore: That's right. You notice that the handwriting doesn't match? How Mr. Garfield's handwriting is totally different from your name there?

Justin: I see that.

Wedmore: What I figure is, Mr. Garfield wrote the check, but left blank who it was to be made out to. Some people, they'll just make it to Cash, or fill in their name themselves. Is that what you did?

Justin: I didn't write my name there.

Wedmore: You didn't?

Justin: No way.

Wedmore: But, hang on . . . the handwriting on the check looks just about identical to these signatures you just did for me.

Justin: I didn't write my name there. Keisha must have done it.

Wedmore: What, you think she put a pen in your hand and wrote your name in while you were unconscious?

Justin: She must have copied it.

Wedmore: From what?

Justin: I don't know. My driver's license? It's probably on that.

Wedmore: That part of your license—we looked—is so worn off you can barely even see it. You know what this looks like, don't you, Justin?

Justin: This is bullshit.

Wedmore: You went to see Mr. Garfield. You gave him Keisha Ceylon's card as a reference, said you were an associate of hers, that you had a vision about his wife. Garfield must have panicked, thought maybe you actually knew he was involved in her death. Something went wrong. He attacked you, and you stabbed him in the eye with the knitting needle. We can put you at the scene, Justin. The footprints outside the window. Your prints on the window frame. Did you look inside before, to check if he was there, or after, to see the mess you'd left behind? We found money with what's likely to be Garfield's blood on it, in your pocket. And finally, Garfield's bloody check, made out to yourself, in your own hand, in that same pocket. That looks kind of bad, don't you think, Justin?

Justin: She did it. I'm telling you. She went there, she tried to get money out of Garfield. She stabbed him in the eye and killed him.

Wedmore: And you know this how?

Justin: Like I said, I followed her there. I was watching through the window.

Wedmore: So you admit you were at the scene.

Justin: Outside! Not inside.

Wedmore: Then how did you get this check? Signed by Mr. Garfield. Made out to you, in your own handwriting?

Justin: I . . . I . . .

Wedmore: If you've got something physical, something that puts Keisha there instead of you, let me have it.

Justin: She was all bloody! Search her house for her clothes.

Wedmore: We did that, Justin. Didn't find anything. Her house, her car looked clean.

Justin: Then she cleaned up! People do that after they kill someone! They clean up!

Wedmore: Is that what you did, Justin? Got all cleaned up after you killed Mr. Garfield?

Justin: I want that lawyer.

THIRTY-FOUR

"So you're going to come to San Francisco with me?" Matthew asked his mother.

"Yeah, but we're not going to stay with my cousin," Keisha said. "What I'm thinking is, we find a place to stay, maybe not right in the city, 'cause it's expensive there, but just outside. See what it's like, maybe even move there."

"I don't know," the boy said.

"I think we need a fresh start," she said. "I can't even go back into that house after what happened there. We're never spending another night in that place."

"Will someone get all my stuff?"

"I'm going in just long enough to pack," Keisha said. She still had Gail's five thousand dollars. She was entitled to that money. It wasn't evidence she had to get rid of. Not like that fragment of an endorsed check Justin's parents had given her, with his signature on the back. She'd flushed that down the toilet before the police arrived, after she'd copied his signature onto the blank check Garfield had written her that morning. All those fake signatures she'd put on Social Security checks for her mom had paid off.

She'd cut it fine. Justin started waking up seconds after she'd planted the money and the check in the pockets of his jacket. So far, the story was hanging together. They had more on him than they did on her. And Justin's parents hadn't pushed yet to have her charged with scamming them. Maybe they had enough on their plate right now, getting a lawyer to defend him on two counts of murder. Or maybe Marcia Taggart didn't want it made public how she and her husband had been duped.

Not just by Keisha, but by her own son.

It seemed like a good time to get out of town. Start over. Turn her life around. Get a job. Maybe she could work at one of those makeup counters in a big department store. She'd be okay with secretarial work, too. Keisha was organized, she could run someone's office, do correspondence, stuff like that.

And if it took a while to get a decent job, she could always, temporarily—not forever, that was for sure—read a few fortunes, she supposed. Check an astrological chart for someone.

If she got really pressed, help someone get in touch with a dead loved one.

Or even someone who was, you know, un-accounted for at the moment.

Tell people what they wanted to hear.

Give them *hope*.

Girl has to make a living.

Acknowledgments

Never Saw it Coming has its origins in a novella I wrote called *Clouded Vision*, which was part of the Quick Reads line-up of short novels designed to encourage reluctant readers to get themselves lost in a book. I want to thank the Quick Reads folks, and everyone else involved in promoting literacy. That includes a lot of people, including publishers, booksellers, the folks who organize World Book Day, teachers, librarians, and most of all, parents who instil a love of reading in their children. Hats off to all of you.

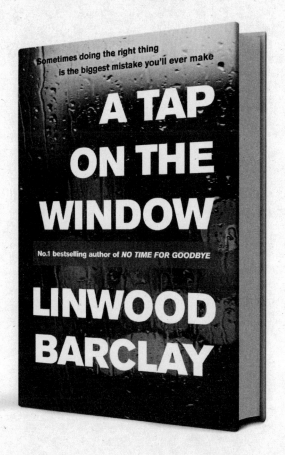

ONE

A middle-aged guy would have to be a total fool to pick up a teenage girl standing outside a bar with her thumb sticking out. Not that bright on her part, either, when you think about it. But right now, we're talking about my stupidity, not hers.

She was standing there at the curb, her stringy blond, rain-soaked hair hanging in her face, the neon glow from the COORS sign in the window of Patchett's Bar bathing her in an eerie light. Her shoulders were hunched up against the drizzle, as if that would some-how keep her warm and dry.

It was hard to tell her age, exactly. Old enough to drive legally and maybe even vote, but not likely old enough to drink. Certainly not here in Griffon, in New York State. The other side of the Lewiston-Queenston Bridge, maybe, in Canada, where the drinking age is nineteen and not twenty-one. But that didn't mean she couldn't have had a few beers at Patchett's. It was gen-erally known your ID was not put through a rigorous examination here. If yours had a picture of Nicole Kid-man on it and you looked more like Penelope Cruz, well, that was good enough for them. Their policy was "Park your butt. What can we getcha?"

The girl, the strap of an oversized red purse slung over her shoulder, had her thumb sticking out, and she was looking at my car as I rolled up to the stop sign at the corner.

Not a chance, I thought. Picking up a male hitchhiker was a bad enough idea, but picking up a teenage girl was monumentally dumb. Guy in his early forties gives a lift to a girl less than half his age on a dark, rainy night. There were more ways for that to go wrong than I could count. So I kept my eyes straight ahead as I put my foot on the brake. I was about to give the Accord some gas when I heard a tapping on the passenger window.

I glanced over, saw her there, bending over, looking at me. I shook my head but she kept on rapping.

I powered down the window far enough to see her eyes and the top half of her nose. "Sorry," I said, "I can't—"

"I just need a lift home, mister," she said. "It's not that far. There's some sketchy guy in that pickup over there. He's been giving me the eye and—" Her eyes popped. "Shit, aren't you Scott Weaver's dad?"

And then everything changed.

"Yeah," I said. I had been.

"Thought I recognized you. You probably wouldn't even know me, but, like, I've seen you pick up Scott at school and stuff. Look, I'm sorry. I'm letting rain get into your car. I'll see if I can get a—"

I didn't see how I could leave one of Scott's friends standing there in the rain.

"Get in," I said.

"You're sure?"

4

"Yeah." I paused, allowed myself one more second to get out of this. Then: "It's okay."

"God, thanks!" she said, opened the door and slid into the seat, moving a cell phone from one hand to the other, slipping the purse off her shoulder and tucking it down by her feet. The dome light was a lightning flash, on and off in a second. "Jeez, I'm soaked. Sorry about your seat."

She was wet. I didn't know how long she'd been there, but it had been long enough for rivulets of water to be running down her hair and onto her jacket and jeans. The tops of her thighs looked wet, making me wonder whether someone driving by had splashed her.

"Don't worry about it," I said as she buckled her seat belt. I was still stopped, waiting for directions. "I go straight, or turn, or what?"

"Oh yeah." She laughed nervously, then shook her head from side to side, flinging droplets of water like a spaniel coming out of a lake. "Like, you're supposed to know where I live. Duh. Just keep going straight."

I glanced left and right, then proceeded through the intersection.

"So you were a friend of Scott's?" I asked.

She nodded, smiled, then grimaced. "Yeah, he was a good guy."

"What's your name?"

"Claire."

"Claire?" I stretched the name out, inviting her to provide a last name. I was wondering if she was someone I'd already checked out online. I really hadn't had a good look at her face yet.

5

"Yep," she said. "Like Chocolate *E. Claire.*" She laughed nervously. She moved the cell phone from her left to right hand, then rested the empty hand on her left knee. There was a bad scratch on the back, just below the knuckles, about an inch long, the skin freshly grazed and raw, just this side of bleeding.

"You hurt yourself, Claire?" I asked, nodding downward.

The girl looked at her hand. "Oh shit, I hadn't even noticed that. Some idiot staggering around Patchett's bumped into me and I caught my hand on the corner of a table. Kinda smarts." She brought her hand up to her face and blew on the wound. "Guess I'll live," she said.

"You don't quite look old enough to be a customer," I said, giving her a reproachful look mixed with a smirk.

She caught the look and rolled her eyes. "Yeah, well."

Neither of us said anything for half a mile or so. The cell phone, as best I could see in the light from my dash, was trapped screen down beneath her hand on her right thigh. She leaned forward to look into the mirror mounted on the passenger door.

"That guy's really riding your bumper," she said.

Headlight glare reflected off my rearview mirror. The vehicle behind us was an SUV or truck, with lights mounted high enough to shine in through my back window. I tapped the brakes just enough to make my taillights pop red, and the driver backed off. Claire kept glancing in the mirror. She seemed to be taking a lot of interest in a tailgater.

"You okay, Claire?" I asked.

"Hmm? Yeah, I'm cool, yeah."

"You seem kind of on edge."

She shook her head a little too aggressively.

"You're sure?" I asked, and as I turned to look at her she caught my eye.

"Positive," she said.

She wasn't a very good liar.

We were on Danbury, a four-lane road, with a fifth down the center for left turns, that was lined with fast-food joints and a Home Depot and a Walmart and a Target and half a dozen other ubiquitous outlets that make it hard to know whether you're in Tucson or Tallahassee.

"So," I said, "how'd you know Scott?"

Claire shrugged. "Just, you know, school. We didn't really hang out that much or anything, but I knew him. I was real sad about what happened to him."

I didn't say anything.

"I mean, like, all kids do dumb shit, right? But most of us, nothing really bad ever happens."

"Yeah," I said.

"When was it, again?" she asked. "'Cause, like, it seems like it was only a few weeks ago."

"It'll be two months tomorrow," I said. "August twenty-fifth."

"Wow," she said. "But, yeah, now that I think of it, there was no school at the time. 'Cause usually everyone would be talking about it in class and in the halls and stuff, but that never happened. By the time we got back, everyone had sort of forgotten." She put her left hand to her mouth and glanced apologetically at me. "I didn't mean it like that."

7

"That's okay."

There were a lot of things I wanted to ask her. But the questions would seem heavy-handed, and I'd known her less than five minutes. I didn't want to come on like someone from Homeland Security. I'd used Scott's list of Facebook friends as something of a guide since the incident, and while I'd probably seen this girl on it, I couldn't quite place her yet. But I also knew that "friendship" on Facebook meant very little. Scott had friended plenty of people he really didn't know at all, including well-known graphic novel artists and other minor celebrities who still handled their own FB pages.

I could figure out who this girl was later. Another time maybe she'd answer a few questions about Scott for me. Giving her a lift in the rain might buy me some future goodwill. She might know something that didn't seem important to her that could be very helpful to me.

Like she could read my mind, she said, "They talk about you."

"Huh?"

"Like, you know, kids at school."

"About me?"

"A little. They already knew what you do. Like, your job. And they know what you've been doing lately."

I suppose I shouldn't have been surprised.

She added, "I don't know anything, so there's no point in asking."

I took my eyes off the rain-soaked road a second to look at her, but said nothing.

The corner of her mouth went up. "I could tell you were thinking about it." She seemed to be reflecting on something, then said, "Not that I blame you or anything, for what you've been doing. My dad, he'd probably do the same. He can be pretty righteous and principled about some things, although not *everything*." She turned slightly in her seat to face me. "I think it's wrong to judge people until you know everything about them. Don't you? I mean, you have to understand that there may be things in their background that make them see the world differently. Like, my grandmother—she's dead now—but she was always saving money, right up until she died at, like, ninety years old, because she'd been through the Depression, which I'd never even heard of, but then I looked it up. You probably know about the Depression, right?"

"I know about the Depression. But believe it or not, I did not live through it."

"Anyway," Claire said, "we always thought Grandma was cheap, but the thing was, she just wanted to be ready in case things got really bad again. Could you pull into Iggy's for a second?"

"What?"

"Up there." She pointed through the windshield.

I knew Iggy's. I just didn't understand why she wanted me to pull into Griffon's landmark ice cream and burger place. It had been here for more than fifty years, or so the locals told me, and even hung in after McDonald's put up its golden arches half a mile down the street. Folks around here who liked a Big Mac over all other burgers would still swing by here for Iggy's signature hand-cut, sea-salted french fries and real ice cream milk shakes.

I'd committed myself to giving this girl a ride home, but a spin through the Iggy's drive-through window seemed a bit much.

Before I could object, she said, "Not for, like, food. My stomach feels a bit weird all of a sudden—beer doesn't always agree with me, you know—and it's bad enough I've got your car wet. I wouldn't want to puke in it, too."

I hit the blinker and pulled up to the restaurant, head-lights bouncing off the glass and into my eyes. Iggy's lacked some of the spit and polish of a McDonald's or Burger King—its menu boards still featured black plastic letters fitted into grooved white panels—but it had a decent-sized eating area, and even at this time of night there were customers. A disheveled man with an oversize backpack, who gave every indication of being a homeless person looking for a place to get in out of the rain, was drinking a coffee. A couple of tables over, a woman was divvying up french fries between two girls, both in pink pajamas, neither of whom could have been older than five. What was the story there? I came up with one that involved an abusive father who'd had too much to drink. They'd come here until they were sure he'd passed out and it was safe to go home.

Before I'd come to a stop, Claire was looping the strap of her purse around her wrist, gathering everything together like she was planning a fast getaway.

"You sure you're okay?" I asked, putting the car in park. "I mean, other than feeling sick?"

"Yeah—yeah, sure." She forced a short laugh. I was aware of some headlights swinging past me as Claire pulled on the door handle. "Be right back." She leapt out and slammed the door.

She raised her purse in front of her face as a shield against the rain as she ran for the door. She disappeared into the back, where the restrooms were located. I glanced over at a black pickup, its windows tinted so heavily I couldn't make out who was driving, that had pulled in half a dozen spots over.

My eyes went back to the restaurant. Here I was, late at night, waiting for a girl I hardly knew—a teenage girl at that—to finish throwing up after an evening of underage drinking. I knew better than to have allowed myself to get into this position. But after she'd mentioned that some guy in a pickup was putting the moves—

Pickup?

I glanced again at the black truck, which actually might have been dark blue or gray—hard to tell in the rain. If anyone had gotten out of it and entered Iggy's, I hadn't noticed.

What I should have done, before she'd gotten into my car, was tell Claire to call her own parents. Let them come get her.

But then she'd gone and mentioned Scott.

I got out my cell, checked to see whether I had any e-mails. I didn't, but the effort helped kill ten seconds. I hit 88.7 on the radio presets, the NPR station out of Buffalo, but couldn't concentrate on anything anyone was saying.

The girl had been in there five minutes. How long did it take to toss your cookies? You went in, you did your thing, splashed some water on your face, and came back out.

Maybe Claire was sicker than she'd realized. It was possible she'd made a mess of herself and needed extra time to clean up.

Great.

I rested my hand on the ignition key, wanting to turn it. *You could just go.* She had a cell phone. She could call someone else to come and get her. I could head home. This girl wasn't my responsibility.

Except that wasn't true. Once I'd agreed to give her a ride, to see that she got home safely, I'd made her my responsibility.

I took another look at the pickup. Just sitting there.

I scanned the inside of the restaurant again. The homeless guy, the woman with the two girls. Now, a boy and girl in their late teens sitting in a booth by the window, sharing a Coke and some chicken fingers. And a man with jet-black hair, in a brown leather jacket, was standing at the counter, his back to me, placing an order.

Seven minutes.

How would it look, I wondered, if this girl's parents showed up now, trying to find her? And discovered me, local snoop-for-hire Cal Weaver, waiting here for her? Would they believe I was just driving her home? That I'd agreed to give her a ride because she knew my son? That my motives were pure?

If I were them, I wouldn't have bought it. And my motives hadn't been entirely pure. I had been wondering whether to try and get some information about

Scott out of her, although I'd quickly abandoned that idea.

The hope of getting her to answer some questions wasn't what kept me here now. I just couldn't abandon a young girl out on this strip, at this time of night. Certainly not without telling her I was leaving.

I decided to go in and find her, make certain she was okay, then tell her to find her way home from here. Give her cab fare if she didn't have anyone else she could call. I got out of the Honda, went into the restaurant, scanned the seats I hadn't been able to see from my outdoor vantage point, just in case Claire was sitting down for a moment. When I didn't find her at any of the tables, I approached the restroom doors at the back, which were steps away from another glass door that led outside.

I hesitated outside the door marked WOMEN, screwed up my nerve, then pushed the door open half an inch.

"Claire? Claire, you okay?"

There was no answer.

"It's me. Mr. Weaver."

Nothing. Not from Claire or anyone else. So I pushed the door open a good foot, cast my eye across the room. A couple of sinks, wall-mounted hand dryer, three stalls. The doors, all closed, were painted a dull tan and bubbling with rust at the hinges. They stopped a foot from the floor, and I didn't notice any feet beneath any of them.

I took a couple of steps, extended an arm and gently touched the door of the first stall. The door, not locked, swung open lazily. I don't know what the hell I was expecting to find. I could tell before I'd opened the door there was no one in there. And then the thought flashed across my mind: what if someone *had* been in there? Claire, or someone else?

This was not a smart place for me to be hanging around.

I exited the bathroom, strode quickly through the restaurant, looking for her. Homeless guy, woman with kids—

The man in the brown leather jacket, the one who'd been ordering food last time I saw him, was gone.

"Son of a bitch," I said.

When I got outside, the first thing I noticed was an empty parking space where the black pickup used to be. Then I saw it. Turning back onto Danbury, flicker on, waiting for a break in the traffic. It wasn't possible to tell, with those tinted windows, whether anyone was in the car besides the driver.

The truck found an opening and took off south, in the direction of Niagara Falls, the engine roaring, back tires spinning on wet pavement.

Could this have been the truck Claire'd been referring to when I allowed her to jump in at Patchett's? If it was, had we been followed? Was the driver the man in the leather jacket? Had he grabbed Claire and taken her with him? Or had she decided he was less threatening than she'd originally thought, and now was going to favor him with the opportunity to drive her home?

Goddamn it.

My heart pounded. I'd lost Claire. I hadn't wanted her in the first place, but I was panicked now that I

14

didn't know where she was. My mind raced while I worked out a plan. Follow the truck? Call the police? Forget the whole damn thing ever happened?

Follow the truck.

Yeah, that seemed the most logical thing. Catch up to it, come up alongside, see if I could catch a glimpse of the girl, make sure she was—

There she was.

Sitting in my car. In the passenger seat, shoulder strap already in place. Blond hair hanging over her eyes.

Waiting for me.

I took a couple of breaths, walked over, got in, slammed the door. "Where the hell were you?" I asked as I dropped into the seat, the interior lights on for three seconds tops. "You were in there so long I was starting to worry."

She stared out the passenger window, her body leaning away from me. "Came out the side door I guess when you were going in." Almost muttering, her voice rougher than before. Throwing up must have taken a toll on her throat.

"You gave me a hell of a start," I said. But there didn't seem much point in reprimanding her. She wasn't my kid, and in a few minutes she'd be home.

I backed the car out, then continued heading south on Danbury.

She kept leaning up against her door, like she was trying to stay as far away from me as possible. If she was wary of me now, why hadn't she been before she'd gone into Iggy's? I couldn't think of anything I'd done to make her fearful. Was it because I'd run into the restaurant looking for her? Had I crossed some kind of line?

There was something else niggling at me, something other than what I might have done. It was something I'd seen, when the light came on inside the car for those five seconds while my door was open.

Things that were only now registering.

First, her clothes.

They were dry. Her jeans weren't darkened with dampness. It wasn't like I could reach over now and touch her knee to see whether it was wet, but I was pretty sure. She couldn't have stripped down in the bathroom and held her jeans up to the hot-air hand dryer, could she? I could barely get those things to blow the water off my hands. Surely they couldn't dry out denim.

But there was more. More disconcerting than the dry clothes. Maybe what I'd thought I'd seen I hadn't seen at all. After all, the light was on for only those few seconds.

I needed to turn it back on to be certain.

I fingered the dial by the steering column that flicked on the dome light. "Sorry," I said. "Just had this thought I left my sunglasses at the Home Depot." I fumbled with my right hand in the small storage area at the head of the console. "Oh yeah, there they are."

And I turned the light back off. It was on long enough for me to be sure.

Her left hand. It was uninjured.

There was no cut.